Cutting Up the Competition

Horror High Series: Book Two

By Carissa Ann Lynch

Cutting Up the Competition

Limitless Publishing, LLC
Kailua, HI 96734
www.limitlesspublishing.com

Formatting: Limitless Publishing

ISBN-13: 978-1-68058-637-4
ISBN-10: 1-68058-637-8

Dedication

To all of the cheerleaders and coaches out there.
And to my cheerleaders in life:
Violet, Dexter, Tristian, and Shannon.
Our family is the best team a girl could ask for.

Chapter One

Amanda

I used to think going to Harrow High would make me feel "normal." I would blend in, make a few friends, but mostly…life would be quiet.

But that was all before my lovely new school got nicknamed "Horror High," and all my plans of fading in the background hit the proverbial shit fan.

At least I'm in my element now because my whole life, all I've ever known is drama and chaos. No quiet moments for this girl…

I moved here last year because my drug-addicted mother could no longer take care of me and my psychopathic father was shot down by police after murdering six people in a bank when I was the ripe old age of ten. It sounds crazy, I know, but it's all true—I swear. Sometimes I wish it wasn't.

The craziest part of all this is that I don't seem so weird anymore. I fit in perfectly at Horror High. I'm not sure if that should make me feel scared or better about my current surroundings…

Living with my Grandma Mimi has been interesting, to say the least. She is a kooky, sometimes manic, but always bizarre former Vegas showgirl that just turned ninety last fall. She hasn't ventured out of her house in nearly ten years with the exception of one day last season when she shocked me and the entire town by showing up at a basketball game where I was cheering. If my year hasn't sounded strange enough to you yet, keep listening.

Last year I made the Harrow Varsity cheerleading squad, along with my best friends Dakota and Sydney. Well, Sydney hasn't always been a friend of mine...but we're best friends now.

Despite the sheer awesomeness of getting selected for the team, a girl who was insanely jealous of our accomplishments actually stalked us and nearly murdered Sydney. Sounds crazy, right? Rest assured—that maniac was arrested for her crimes, and she's safely tucked away in a juvenile detention center far away from Harrow Hill and us.

At least that's what we thought...

Dakota calls our *new* stalker "The Prankster" because he or she has been calling us off and on all summer, making vague childish threats in a lame robotic voice. We've agreed—it's a copycat, probably one of our classmates trying to upset us and fuel the drama flames from last year's incident.

You might ask: *Who would do such a thing?*

My answer to that is lots of people. This town is full of weirdos and girls who love to hate on us— especially because we're cheerleaders.

Had enough of my drama yet? Well, hold on to

your seats because the real drama is about to begin. Today is the first day of school, and unlike last year, I'm feeling a bit more confident because this time around I'm a sophomore instead of a freshman. The first day is always the most exciting and I'm only two years shy of running this place!

After all the insanity of last school year, this year is bound to be better. It's already getting off to a good start because my best friend, Dakota, got her driver's license last January, and three days ago, her mom and dad surprised her with a new car. It's a used red Chevrolet Cavalier convertible from 1987. It has a dent on the passenger's side, racing stripes that are actually a pattern of faded paint, and a cloth top that leaks when it rains. Basically perfect, in my opinion.

I'm old enough to get my license too, but since I don't have a car, what's the point? I'm just super excited that Dakota can drive us to and from school each day instead of being forced to take the bus.

We whipped into the school parking lot, the top to the Cavalier down, a One Direction song blaring from the speakers, sending shockwaves up my back. I don't know if I've ever felt this cool before.

Dakota selected a parking space in the back, which is usually a segment of the lot reserved for seniors, but today it didn't matter. We're cheerleaders. We're sophomores. *We make our own damn rules.*

In the spirit of being cool, I climbed over the side of the convertible instead of using the door to get out. Isn't that what the cool kids did in the 80s' movies?

3

Dakota's boyfriend, Andy McGraw, followed my lead and climbed out from the passenger seat. Dakota and Andy have been dating since last year. He's also a sophomore. They're basically the most perfect couple I've ever seen—all smiles and hand holding and back rubs…yuck.

I won't say that I'm jealous, but I do envy the closeness they share. I've really, truly never been close to anyone. That is, until I met Dakota last year and learned what it is to have real, dependable friends.

Sydney—my other bestie—being her usual elegant and classy self, opened the car door slowly and stepped out from the back, whipping her velvety black hair around with dramatic flair. Sydney's got legs for days and today she's wearing a red cotton dress and dainty leggings that look stunning with her long mane of hair that stretches down the length of her back. Dakota was right behind her and I quickly followed, forming a line with both girls.

The three of us marched toward the door with Andy in our wake.

We were walking like we owned the place.

Maybe this year, we will.

Chapter Two

Harrow High is a fairly small school, with only two hundred students comprising its graduating class last year.

As I walked through the entrance, there were swarms of students I recognized, dozens of my fellow sophomores and upperclassmen I remembered from last year. Some of them I still didn't know well.

Unlike me, Dakota and Sydney have lived in this town their whole lives, and I was pretty sure they knew about everyone in the entire school. I noticed clusters of new students too—undoubtedly, this was our new freshman class. I couldn't help wondering which of the girls would show up at cheerleading tryouts today.

Last year, the team was comprised of me, Dakota, and Sydney, as well as three other girls— Genevieve McDermott, Tally Johannsen, and Tamika Rutherford. The three of us and Genevieve would certainly try out again this year, but Tally and Tamika graduated last May.

Although we all had to try out all over again, I felt certain that the four of us would retain our positions on the squad. That meant there were two vacant spots for our new freshman girls. I knew I should be at least a tiny bit worried, but honestly…I wasn't.

Waving goodbye to Sydney and Dakota, I made my way to the west wing of the building, which is where my first class—Chemistry—was held, according to the schedule I'd printed off the school's website. Unlike last year, I was more familiar with the school's layout and confident I could find all of my classes with ease.

As I hustled down the hallway to the chemistry lab, I just happened to glance down a narrow, connecting hallway that *also* happened to be the place where Sydney almost died last year. An involuntary shudder rolled through my body as I thought about that night and the sheer terror I felt in those crucial moments before Sydney was rescued. My body kept moving, but my eyes stayed with that hallway, barely missing a traffic jam of students ahead.

I stopped, sighing as I waited for kids to stop blocking the hallway. My eyes were still drawn down *the* hallway of doom, and I immediately caught a glance of a cute girl with white-blonde hair. She was pacing up and down the hallway frantically, holding a sheet of white paper in front of her nose, most likely her school schedule.

The girl stopped moving, squinted down at the sheet, and then threw up her hands in disgust. Nobody helped me out last year when I was a

6

freshman, and the bell was about to ring, but I couldn't help feeling the urge to help her. *Who knows? Maybe I'll turn out to be a real do-gooder this year...*

"Dang it, Amanda," I scolded myself. Veering right, I turned straight toward the dreaded hallway to help her.

"What classroom are you trying to find?" The white-blonde girl whipped around to see who was asking. Letting out a sigh of relief, she pointed at the first line on her schedule sheet.

"I need to get to Chemistry. It's supposed to be in room seventeen in the west wing, but there are no rooms with the number seventeen on them in this hallway." She thrust the paper at my chest.

I smiled tightly. "You're in the right wing, but this is the wrong hallway. Nothing good happens in this hallway," I rambled. "Look, I'm going to the same class. Just follow me." I led her to an adjacent hallway, which did in fact, contain room seventeen.

She was carrying a star-printed messenger bag, and I couldn't help but appreciate the sheer number of funky-styled rings lining her fingers. The white hair, dark eye makeup, and alternative accessories created an interesting style on her—one that I coveted.

"Wait a minute. Are you sure you have Chemistry for your first period? I thought freshmen took Biology..." She shook her head, grinning widely to reveal slightly spaced teeth. Somehow, even the odd teeth looked great on her.

"I'm not a freshman. I used to live in Crimson County, which is only a couple towns over. You probably know where I'm talking about. My family and I were going to move to Hawaii 'cause my dad's in the service, but plans changed and we decided to move closer to town. So, I am technically a newbie even though I'm not a freshman. I'm Winter Addams."

She stuck out her ring-clad hand for me to shake. I accepted it, smiling. I could remember all too well what it felt like to be the new girl in town last year, so I could relate with this girl completely. I motioned for her to keep following, and I took her by the arm as we weaved in and out of the crowds.

We pushed our way through one last swarm of students, and then I tapped at the numbered sign on the door with a smile. "Seventeen," I bragged. She grinned back gratefully. We slid into two seats in the back row, just in time for the bell.

I looked at this new strange girl and couldn't help wondering if we'd become friends this year. Girls we passed gave her dirty, jealous looks while the boys stared at her, some of them catcalling. New or not, she certainly wouldn't go unnoticed.

What would I have done last year if Dakota hadn't befriended me when she did? Luckily, Dakota and I were next door neighbors, so we were able to get chummy over the summer before school started.

I made a decision right then: to throw Winter a bone and try to help her feel welcome at Harrow Hill. She'd fit in just fine with Dakota, and Sydney too. They say three's a crowd, so why not add a fourth bestie to our clique? I couldn't see any good reasons why not.

Chapter Three

Second period of the day was British Literature, and I was pleased to see Sydney perched on a seat in the back of the room. I was even more excited to see Coach Dolly Davis standing at the front, clearing red arithmetic problems from the class before off the dry erase board.

In addition to teaching, Coach Davis is the cheerleading coach. She coached me last year when I was a freshman squad member. I had heard plenty of rumors about her approach to teaching versus coaching sports. Supposedly, she was much more lax on her students than her team members. I hoped like hell that rumor was true because English wasn't my strong suit. I was more of a science and math kind of girl.

"How's your day so far?" I took a seat next to Sydney, smiling giddily at my friend.

"As well as can be expected. I need a few more weeks of summer." She yawned, stretching her long, graceful arms up over her head. "How's your day going so far?"

9

"Great! I met a cool new girl in Chemistry—" Before I could say more, Winter herself darted inside the classroom, finding a seat near the front moments before the bell rang.

"That's her." I pointed her out to Sydney. Winter looked back at me and waved.

"Do you think she'll try out for cheerleading?" Sydney whispered as Coach Davis took her stance at the front of the room, leaning on the edge of her desk. I shrugged, focusing on the Coach.

"Welcome to Brit Lit. My name is Mrs. Davis, or some of you may know me as Coach…" She winked at Sydney and I.

But her introductions were cut short by the light sounds of giggling in the hallway, and then Dakota strolled through the doorway, waving her goodbyes to Andy.

Those two lovebirds, I thought, rolling my eyes with a grin. Dakota slid into the first available seat, muttering a few embarrassed apologies to Coach Davis while pulling out her paper and pens. Coach Davis raised her eyebrows, then picked up where she left off.

Dakota spotted me and Sydney a few minutes later and waved back at the both of us. It was awesome being in the same class together!

But as she turned back around to face Coach Davis, her eyes locked on Winter, who was sitting a couple seats to her right.

Her mouth went slack, her expression hardening. It was a cross between anger and disbelief.

I tried to catch her gaze once more, intent on giving her a questionable look, my way of asking what this was all about. But she kept her focus on Winter throughout most of the period. It gave me the creeps, honestly.

What was going on between those two? Why was Dakota acting so strangely toward the new girl? For reasons unknown to me, I felt a sudden, unexpected, protectiveness over Winter. I had to figure out why Dakota was mean mugging her for no apparent reason!

Chapter Four

It didn't take long to receive my answer. As soon as the bell rang, Dakota pulled Sydney and I aside right outside of the classroom door. "Winter Addams is a student here now!" She gave us this look, as though we were supposed to be shocked by this sudden random declaration.

"I know who she is. I met her in Chem Lab. She seems really nice," I responded defensively. Dakota stared at me as though I was the Anti-Christ. Clearing her throat, she said, "Winter Addams is Andy's ex-girlfriend. She's the one I caught him making out with last year, when we first started talking. Supposedly, she's moving to—"

"Hawaii," I finished for her. "Her dad is in the military and his orders changed. They're sticking around for a while. They moved from Crimson County." I started to say more, but Dakota's once angry face was now flushed a reddish-purple hue, like she might explode with rage at any second. It was a side of her I hadn't seen before.

"If you guys want to be friends with her, then

12

fine. But she's *my* worst enemy!" Dakota stormed off huffily, moving away from us down the hall. I looked at Sydney, but she was quick to rush ahead, chasing after her best friend. I stood there, clogging up the hallway, feeling completely defeated.

Now, more than ever, I realized how truly alone I still was. Dakota and Sydney had been best friends their entire lives, and I only became a part of their world last year. They would always stick together, choosing each other over me, and as much as I hated to admit it, I was number three on the totem pole. Obviously, whenever Dakota was mad at me, Sydney would naturally follow suit, and vice versa. I felt my own face heat up. I moved ahead, eager to get to my next class.

Next was Childhood Development, and unlike the normal rows of desks in the other classrooms, this room consisted of four chunky tables surrounded by chairs. There were only a few other students in the room, so I picked an empty table, slumping down and tossing my backpack on top of the table in front of me.

It was only day one of sophomore year, and I was already prepared to call it a day. Unfortunately, the day's end was nowhere near, considering the fact that I still had half a day ahead of me and afterschool tryouts.

I wondered how it would be on the squad this year if I wasn't friends with Dakota or Sydney. Sure, we'd all get over this insignificant little squabble but what about the rest of the year? If we were already fighting on the first day, then I wasn't sure how well the rest of the year would go. Other students were filing inside, filling up chairs at the tables. Just when I thought I might luck out and get my table all to myself, the chair beside me screeched painfully and a handsome, shaggy-haired boy squeezed in the seat right next to me. *With so many other seats around, did he really have to choose the one directly beside me?* I wondered, feeling annoyed. But then he glanced at me. Smiled softly. My foul mood disappeared completely.

His skin was the color of honey-covered toast. "Hi," he said simply, and then turned toward the elderly, frumpy teacher who'd just stepped inside. It was obvious to me now that he had sat down so close because he wanted to be near me. Perhaps I wasn't going to be so lonely this year after all!

***

Forty-five minutes later, I was sliding my folders into my backpack when he finally said more than one word to me. I could feel him standing there beside me, staring at me expectantly. "Hey, I'm Jordan." His voice was quiet, but confident.

I swung my backpack over my shoulders and smiled up at him, feeling uncharacteristically shy. He seemed taller standing up, and even more attractive than my peripheral vision had let on.

"Amanda Loxx." I stood there, wringing my hands together awkwardly. For a moment, a silence ensued between us, and I cleared my throat to relieve it. "I don't think I've ever seen you before. Are you new here?" I was trying to sound polite, but I really wanted to know—something about him made me curious. He certainly looked too tall and mature to be a freshman.

"I'm not a freshman, if that's what you're thinking," he said, reading my thoughts exactly. "I'm actually a junior. My last school in Crimson County didn't offer any courses in child development, so I'm taking this as an elective. My mom is always saying that if I knew how difficult it was to raise a baby, then maybe I'd think twice about having so many girlfriends. Did you know that we get to carry one of those plastic babies that whine and cry all the time?"

I was too stuck on the fact that he said he was from Crimson County to pay attention to the rest of his words. "Did you say you were from Crimson?" I cut off his rant about artificial infants.

"Yeah, I was supposed to attend high school in Hawaii this year, hanging out on the beach...talk about a bummer, eh?"

"Wait. Did you say Hawaii?" I asked incredulously. This was all sounding vaguely familiar.

The rest of the students had emptied out of the room, and grumpy Mrs. Brooch was staring at us blankly from her desk, tapping her pencil rudely. "Get to your next class, please," she grumbled. We giggled and headed for the door.

"You see, the weird thing is...I met this new girl today who was also supposed to move to Hawaii—" Based on the knowing smile that spread across his face, Jordan already knew who I was talking about.

"So, you met my sister then," he stated matter-of-factly.

"Your sister?" I asked disbelievingly. He nodded, trotting down the hallway beside me. I noticed small herds of girlish faces, staring at Jordan as though he were eye candy. I moved a few inches closer to him, turning up my nose in their direction.

"It's cool that you've already made friends with my sister. Since you guys are already friends, maybe we can hang out more too," he suggested hopefully.

"That sounds really...wonderful," I murmured dreamily, sticking right by his side.

"Speaking of my sister, we're supposed to meet up for lunch. You want to hang out with us?" Just as the question left his lips, I saw Sydney and Dakota up ahead, making a beeline for the back of the lunch line. I let out a groan.

Dakota was going to be so pissed at me if she saw me hanging out with Winter at lunch. I hated to risk losing her friendship forever. But as I looked over at this tall, handsome stranger, I couldn't help myself. "I would absolutely love to," I said, sticking out my chin flirtatiously.

Chapter Five

The lunch room was filled with my classmates' chatter and sounds of heavy, plastic trays sliding across the Formica counters of the lunch tables. There were nearly twenty tables with windows on each side, and I was sitting in a seat near the back, hiding from Sydney and Dakota. The truth is that I felt terrible for avoiding them, especially after my spat with Dakota in Brit Lit this morning, but here I was anyway—sitting with my two new friends, Winter and Jordan Addams.

Winter was still recovering from the shock that her brother and I had hit it off right after she and I became friends. As I shoved bland tasting spaghetti noodles into my mouth from my lunch tray, I stared at the two siblings. They didn't look anything alike. Winter was fair-skinned with that white-blonde hair and she stood out like a sore thumb, especially next to her brother, who was sporting a dark tan and even darker shaggy locks. She must dye her hair, I realized foolishly.

I, for one, have never dyed my hair. Not because

17

I'm above it, but because I've never had anyone to help me do it. When your dad dies tragically and your mom is off doping somewhere, you don't really have many adults to help with everyday things, like hair care.

Winter and Jordan were discussing their class schedules amongst themselves, and to be honest, I was feeling a little left out. Despite their differences in physical appearance, their mannerisms were similar and they seemed to get along perfectly. I felt another slight twinge of jealousy—I'd always dreamt of having a sibling.

"So, did you used to date Andy McGraw?" I blurted out of the blue. Winter's spaghetti-covered fork froze in mid-air.

"How did you know that?" she asked.

"Dakota Densford is my best friend. She recognized you this morning in Brit Lit, and she told me you were Andy's ex. Apparently, you met Dakota last year when she caught the two of you kissing." I said it fast, a hint of a question in my voice.

"Well, for your information, Andy and Dakota were not actually dating yet when we hooked up. His dad and my dad were friends in the Army, and we've known each other since we were toddlers. That day, when I went to see Andy, it was because I'd just learned my dad was going to be stationed in Hawaii. I wanted to tell him goodbye." Winter seemed stiff, nervous.

"Dakota and Andy are pretty serious now." I gave her a warning glance.

"I'm not interested in dating Andy anymore."

Winter sniffed, turning back to poking her food. Jordan was quiet, looking back and forth between us.

"So, in other news," he said, drawing out his words to get our attention, "I'm going to talk to Coach Purnell after school today about possibly joining the basketball team."

"That's great, Jordan!" Winter squealed. "He's such a good basketball player," she said to me, smiling proudly at her brother. "Since we didn't know we were going to be students here over the summer, he didn't have the opportunity to try out. But he was the best player on the team in Crimson County," she further explained. I nodded understandably.

"Yeah, basketball tryouts are always in the summer. But cheerleading tryouts are on the first day of school. Today." I glanced up at the cafeteria clock, remembering for the first time since this morning. "If you make the team, you might get to see me. I was on the squad last year, so I should be able to nail a spot again this year." I winked at Jordan and he smiled right back.

Winter let out an excited whoop, wriggling around in her seat happily. "I'm trying out too!" She clapped her hands together. "We can be besties, *and* cheer buddies!" she exclaimed, grinning wildly.

"Dakota's on the squad too," I said, mostly talking to myself.

How was this going to work? If my best friend and new friend were arch-nemeses, and I was caught in the middle, then this couldn't bode well for me.

That's ridiculous, I thought instantly. *We're not in third grade; we're sophomores now, for goodness sake! I shouldn't have to pick sides*. But that's when I saw Dakota and Sydney glaring at me from across the lunchroom. You'd think I'd killed someone by the dirty looks they were sending. I suddenly realized that just because I didn't have to pick sides, didn't mean they wouldn't try to make me…

Chapter Six

My last classes of the day were a series of blurred events; my garbled attempts at reciting the French alphabet, my loathing of all things that have to do with line segments, rays, and types of angles, and my favorite—please note my sarcasm here—the effects of European colonization on the States.

By the time the final bell rang, bringing its usual relief to all students alike, I felt sleepy and irritable. Not to mention the fact that the entire school felt like one huge sweatbox, my paper-thin t-shirt stuck to my chest as I made my way from my locker to the gym for tryouts.

I should have been more exuberant about the upcoming season and the tryouts that lay ahead, but I was dreading a run-in with Dakota and Sydney, and also my new friend, Winter. I was walking against the foot traffic, students scampering down the hallways, headed out to either their own personal vehicles or to catch the bus. But I was headed for the gym.

Students brushed past me rudely, their heavy

backpacks banging against my outer thighs painfully. Since it was day number one of the school year, everyone was wearing the best of their new school gear. I saw lots of skinny jeans, flashy leggings, and every color of Uggs you could imagine.

At my old school, we had to wear these wooly, school-marmish uniforms. *At least at Harrow High, we have options when it comes to school dress,* I reminded myself. There was a code, of course; there always is. But for the most part, Principal Barlow was pretty easygoing when it came to enforcing the dress code rules. And speaking of Principal Barlow, her daughter was standing at the outer edges of the gym entrance, smiling at me brightly.

Brittani Barlow is a total fruitcake—and that's putting it lightly. She's an overachiever when it comes to everything related to academics or sports, but she also has about as much emotional intelligence as a pet rock. Last year, no one was surprised when she made the team. Not only was she Principal's Barlow's daughter, but she was also a damn good cheerleader. However, it was her personality that cost her a spot on the team because she got caught purposefully dropping other cheerleaders in stunts just to lower the field of competitors. After her removal from the team last year, I was a little taken aback by her presence near the gym ten minutes before tryouts.

"Hey, Amanda!" Brittani squealed, walking straight toward me. She clutched me in an awkward embrace before I had a chance to pull away.

"Hi," I answered unsurely, making it sound more

like a question than a greeting. "I'm not trying to be rude, but what are you doing at tryouts, Brittani?"

The smile on her face didn't flicker or fade. "Oh, well...I'm trying out again this year. The principal gave me permission to try again, as long as I'm on my best behavior!" She flashed that wooden smile of hers.

"The *principal*? You mean your *mother*?" I asked bitterly. Brittani let out a creepy bubble of laughter, and said, "Well, of course I'm talking about my mother. I don't see any other principals around here, do you?" She giggled.

"I don't have time for this." I pushed past her, heading through the heavy, metal doors to the gym. I was surprised to see a group of boys stretching in the center of the basketball court. My eyes were immediately drawn to where Jordan stood, bent at the waist stretching his hamstrings and calves. *I guess he's going to be practicing with the team today after all,* I thought, smiling in spite of myself. I knew how badly he wanted to play basketball, and I had to admit to myself that I wanted to see him play this year too.

Mostly, I want to see him in those shorts and sleeveless jersey...

As I passed the boys on my way to the locker room, he looked up at me, smiling widely. I gave him a small wave and couldn't stop myself from grinning. I'd had a few boyfriends in the past, and I'd even had a short-lived fling with one of the basketball players last year, a douche bag named Ronnie...but I'd never felt this girlish or giddy over a boy before, and I sort of liked the fluttering feeling.

Finally breaking eye contact with him, I entered the locker room to dress in my athletic tights and top. The outfit fit snugly over my chest, rear, and hips, and I felt sexy in it. I dabbed on a little pale lipstick—although I knew Coach Davis would find it unnecessary—and I headed to one of the back stalls to blot my lips on toilet paper. *I'll have to remember to get down here early every day. It's kind of nice having the locker room all to myself.*

I could hear the door behind me swing open, other cheerleading hopefuls pouring in. I reached through the half open stall door, grabbing for the toilet paper roll, but then I froze. There was someone inside the stall already, slumped at an awkward angle over the toilet.

I jumped back, then peeked back in, shaking my head from side to side. Sounds of screaming ripped through my eardrums.

It took me a moment to realize it was the shrill sound of my own voice.

Other girls rushed to my side, including Dakota and Sydney.

Someone kicked the stall door all the way open, and we all stared in horror at the girl inside. She was clearly dead, her eyes lifeless, her skin a sullen gray. I didn't want to look but at the same time, I couldn't pull my eyes away from her face. Well, mainly, her nose—or lack of a nose, I should say.

Even in death she looked beautiful. The dead girl was Genevieve McDermott.

Chapter Seven

The next hour passed like a blur. There were screams and shuffling, all of the basketball players and cheerleading hopefuls corralled into a small advanced theatre classroom.

It was hard to believe there were really this many of us.

We were shoulder to shoulder, struggling to see over each other's heads and hear what Principal Barlow was saying.

The police had been called. Harrow High was on lockdown and all of the students remaining at the school were stuck there until the police deemed it safe to go home. Our parents had been called. Unless she called our name, we were ordered to take our usual route home.

I'd lost Dakota and Sydney in the crowd, but now Jordan was standing next to me.

He rubbed my shoulders from behind, hunching his own, as he was nearly a foot taller than me. He leaned down and whispered in my ear. He asked me something, but my mind was somewhere else.

In that locker room…that stall. Genevieve's limp body propped up on the toilet seat. Her skin waxy and dull.

Her butchered face…

I shuddered, my shoulders quivering. Jordan turned me around, pressing me against his own chest. He smelled like aftershave, cologne, and heaven all mixed into one gorgeous scent.

He stroked my hair, staring down into my face. I willed myself not to cry.

"It's okay, Amanda. It's going to be okay. It will all be over soon. The police just want to make sure whoever did this isn't still inside the school, and then we can go."

Unless whoever did this is right here…in this room somewhere, I wanted to say.

"Thank you," I managed to whisper. My voice was hoarse, an after effect of screaming for a half hour straight.

"Detective Simms wants to talk to you." It was Mr. Church, one of the algebra teachers who hadn't made it out of the building before Genevieve's body was found.

"Me? Why me?"

"Because you found her." He tried to smile, an attempt to reassure me. It did nothing to relieve the big ball of anxiety contracting in my abdomen.

Jordan squeezed my arm and nodded. *He's so cute*, I thought, noticing a dimple on his right cheek for the first time. Hard to believe I could think about liking him, or anyone, at a time like this.

Detective Simms was waiting for me, and I followed him out of the room, avoiding the glares of my fellow classmates. Surely no one suspected it was me who hurt Genevieve…

But then I thought about last year…all of the fliers hanging up around school—pictures of my father's mugshot and me. *Like father, like daughter?*—those were the words printed on the flier.

Detective Simms motioned for me to take a seat in an empty classroom. I recognized it as my Biology class from last year.

I sighed. "I don't know what happened to Genevieve. I went into a stall to get a piece of toilet paper to blot my lips, and that's when I found her…dead."

Detective Simms took a seat at the desk next to me.

He stared at me, silently. "I just talked to Dakota and Sydney. Why didn't you guys tell me you were still getting harassing phone calls this summer?"

I tried to swallow down the lump in my throat. "We just figured it was a copycat, someone trying to keep the drama going…plus they haven't called in over a month."

"You should have told me." His face was stern, but not angry.

"I'm sorry," I said, staring at a crude drawing of a big-breasted cheerleader on the desk.

"I need to see your phone." Without hesitation, I reached inside my bag and handed over my iPhone.

"When will I get it back?"

"You can come to the station in a couple days and pick it up then." I nodded, still trying to forget Genevieve's nose. *Who would want to kill her? One*

27

of the other cheerleaders? Someone she'd had a beef with?

And the real question—who did Genevieve not have a beef with? That girl was bitchy as hell...

Despite Genevieve's unlikable personality traits, no one I knew seemed capable of something so horrible. *And why chop off her nose?*

"Was she murdered?" I looked up, staring at Detective Simms' face, trying to read his expression. I heard myself ask the question and realized it sounded stupid. *Of course she was murdered,* I scolded myself. *Last time I checked there's not some rotting nose disease going around that kills healthy teenagers.*

"We won't know until further investigation, but for now...it looks like foul play to me."

He walked me back to the classroom I'd been held in before. Looking around for Jordan, I finally spotted him next to his sister and another girl.

"You want a ride home? They're letting us go. Rumor is, school might be canceled for a few days while they process the crime scene."

I didn't mind the idea of a few days off. All I wanted to do was hide under the covers and forget about strips of flesh stretched against bone. And empty nose sockets...

I shuddered again.

"Amanda. Do you want us to take you home?" Winter repeated. Her voice was soft, comforting. She gave me a sad smile.

I nodded, letting them lead me out of the classroom. Parents were arriving out front and kids were headed to their usual end of the day destinations. Some of them were still waiting for family to pick them up.

I caught a glimpse of the east hallway. It was blocked off with caution tape. Several police officers were clustered outside of the gym. Discussing Genevieve, no doubt.

We had barely made it out to the parking lot when I saw Sydney and Dakota standing near the front entranceway. *Were they waiting for me?*

You would think after what happened to Genevieve, Dakota might forget about our stupid little tiff but instead, she scowled, narrowing her eyes at Winter and shaking her head at me.

I gave her an apologetic look, but kept going. I needed to get home. I needed to process all of this. I didn't care how I got there or who took me, as long as I got there and away from this school.

They don't call it Horror High for nothing...

Chapter Eight

I'd never been so happy to see my Grandma Mimi's house. I was so out of it that I jumped out, forgetting to thank Jordan and Winter for bringing me home.

There was another girl in the car who rode with us. I didn't know who she was, nor did I even think to ask. Normally, I'm pretty polite, but I had a lot on my mind...

Grandma Mimi is pretty strange. She sleeps late, wears makeup to bed, and drinks cocktails off and on all day. She used to be a showgirl in Vegas and supposedly, had a heavy drug problem to boot.

She's my dad's mother—no surprise there—but we never talk about him. He's dead now, which is arguably where he probably deserves to be.

I pulled out my key and lifted it toward the lock. Surprised to find the door slightly open, I pushed it the rest of the way in, tentatively stepping inside. Mimi is a little paranoid and rarely leaves the house, so the door being left open was worrisome. Usually, she kept the house locked tight, like we were protecting Fort Knox or something…

"Grandma?" I shouted, dropping my backpack in the foyer. I peeked in the living room. I expected an intruder or to find Mimi sick on the floor. But what I found was inherently worse.

My mother was sitting on the couch.

Chapter Nine

"What the hell is she doing here?"

"*She* is your mother, and *she* came to see you. We heard about what happened at school. We were both worried sick about you."

I looked back and forth between my mother and Grandma Mimi.

"I'm fine. And I don't want to see her." I headed back out to the foyer to grab my backpack and go upstairs. I suddenly felt the urge to go back to school.

But then I remembered Genevieve's face...

"Honey, please." My mother followed me, her face twisted in pain, the way it always looked when she felt guilty.

I'd been through this routine before. She'd say she was sorry and make amends. She'd stay clean for a few weeks and then she'd disappear—no note, no nothing.

Well, not this time...

"What do you *really* want, Mom...money? Are you getting married again?"

"I wanted to see you, Mandy!" She reached for me, but I jerked away, disgusted by the nickname she had for me. She only called me Mandy when she wanted to manipulate me.

"Well, here I am. And I'm fine. I like it here, so you can go now." I folded my arms across my chest. Childish, I know, but I just couldn't help myself.

Seeing her was the last thing I wanted to deal with after a day like today...

All I really wanted to do was jump under the dusty quilt I kept on my bed, stick my ear buds in, and turn the music up so loud it drowned out the images of Genevieve...

"She's staying for a while." Grandma Mimi stepped out of the living room, shoulder to shoulder with Mom.

Screw both of them, I thought angrily. I grabbed my backpack and walked out the door.

I didn't know where I was going. Dakota lived next door but we were fighting, and even if we weren't, that still seemed too close to my mother.

I jogged toward Heather Street, but going where? I wasn't sure. I didn't know where Jordan and Winter lived, and even if I did, I didn't know them well enough to just show up at their door.

Two streets over, I finally realized where I was headed. Sydney's house.

We weren't as close as Dakota and I, and after today, she was probably pissed at me too. But she was the only other option I could come up with.

I wasn't going back to Grandma Mimi's. Not with that woman still there. Sure, she's my mom and I'm supposed to love her, but she's never done anything but cause me pain.

Her and my stupid dad, I thought bitterly.

I was standing in front of Sydney's house. It was big and fancy, the nicest on the block. Her parents had money, but I'd barely met them. Every once in a while, I'd see Sydney riding home from practice or school in her dad's Mercedes, but I'd never even met the man. Or her mom, for that matter…

Hesitating on the front porch, I was shocked when the door flung open. Sydney stood in the doorframe, her long black hair pulled up in a tight, high ponytail. She was wearing sweats and a faded Harrow High t-shirt, but as usual, she looked like a girl straight from the cover of YM magazine.

"I saw you through the window. I just got home and changed…" Sydney stared at me, her eyes wide and worried.

"I didn't know where else to go. My mom is back and I don't want to see her. And I can't stop thinking about Genevieve. The way her nose was sliced off…"

Sydney ushered me inside, leading me up a lovely, curved staircase with fancy carvings and phony vegetation twisted through its rails.

"My parents aren't here," she said out of the blue, reaching the top and pointing toward her bedroom. I followed her inside a lovely black and white bedroom, fit for a princess with a sparkly chandelier and ornate fixtures.

A large canopy bed sat in the center of the room. Magazines were sprawled across the bed and a neat silver comb set was perfectly lined on the dresser. Somehow this was *exactly* what I'd imagined

Sydney's room to look like.

Her mom and dad worked in stocks, whatever the hell that meant. Clearly, they weren't hurting for money.

Speaking of parents, I wonder how Genevieve's family will react when they find out about their daughter...

I tried to swallow, but couldn't. I tried to breathe, but couldn't. I felt like I was going to have a full blown panic attack and the room just would not stop spinning.

"Sit down. I'll get you some water," Sydney offered, moving me toward the bed and reaching below a fancy entertainment center. She had her own personal fridge hidden below.

I gladly accepted the water, eager to soothe my gravelly throat.

Finally able to catch my breath, I smiled and thanked her. The water tasted good, cleansing.

"I just can't believe Genevieve's dead," Sydney whispered, collapsing on the bed beside me. "I mean, Ashleigh's in jail, so it couldn't be her. Are you really telling me there are *two* crazy people at Harrow—*Horror*—High?" It was a question, but she didn't seem to be asking me in particular.

She stood up, pacing around the room. "Do you think it was Ronnie?" she asked, looking around the room wildly.

"They're still dating, right?" I finished off the water, screwing the cap back on tightly.

Sydney stopped, realizing I was in the room. *Apparently, I'm not the only one freaking out,* I thought, suddenly feeling better.

"I think so," Sydney replied, moving back to the bed beside me.

"Ronnie is an asshole. But I can't see him hurting Genevieve, even if they got in a fight."

Sydney nodded. "But then again, I can't see anyone doing that, can you?"

I thought about it. *No, I couldn't.*

"My parents are out of town. Maybe I should call them, tell them there's a crazy killer on the loose. I don't want to stay home alone!" Sydney whined, jumping up to peer out from her second story bedroom window.

It was my turn to comfort her. "I'll stay the night with you. In fact, *please* let me stay. I don't want to be with my mother right now."

Sydney turned around and smiled. "I haven't had a sleepover in forever. We could make popcorn and watch movies and—"

Suddenly, she seemed to be feeling better. "Just no scary movies, okay?" I flinched at the thought of watching something bloody and gory. *Never again*, I thought. *Not after seeing Genevieve like that today.*

Sydney pursed her lips. "Do reruns of *Buffy the Vampire Slayer* qualify as scary?" I laughed in spite of myself.

"Sounds perfect."

So, for the next six hours, we vegged out on the couch, watching Buffy kick some vampire butt and eating every bit of junk food we could find stashed away in Sydney's immaculate, walk-in pantry.

After the events of today, I thought I'd never feel safe enough to sleep again. But sure enough, we both passed out on the couch sometime after midnight.

We didn't wake up until the next morning, to the sounds of someone banging on the door.

"Syd! Open up! We're going be late!" It was Dakota. *I'd know that nasally voice from anywhere.*

We both jumped up, stumbling over bowls of popcorn and grape soda cans. I made it to the door first.

"They didn't call school off?" I asked, throwing the door open wide. Dakota stared at me, shocked to see me hanging out at her best friend's house. Her eyes narrowed. *I'm getting used to this expression from her...*

She looked over my shoulder at Sydney, who was rushing around to get her backpack and purse. "You let her stay with you?" Dakota asked, obviously *her* meaning *me*.

"My mom showed up again. I don't know what she wants this time, but after what happened yesterday, I just couldn't take it, ya know?" Tears were flowing now. I swiped them away with the back of my hand, feeling foolish.

Dakota's face softened. "Oh, Amanda. I'm so sorry. You could have come over to my house..."

We stood there hugging, our way of making up, I suppose.

"I hate to break up the love fest, but I cannot be late to school. I have to dissect a pig today in advanced bio," Sydney sniffed from behind us. Rolling my eyes, I turned and ran upstairs to get my stuff. Time to head back to *Horror High*.

Chapter Ten

I was surprised school was open today, but I was even more surprised when I walked in and found Mariella Martin—Genevieve's *old* best friend—red-rimmed and crying in the hallway. Students were piled up around her, listening to her talk about Genevieve like they were still best friends.

"And she always knew how to make the best French braid!" Mariella moaned, her bright red curls falling over her face as she sniffled and whined to her classmates. I noticed that a lot of them were freshmen, which meant they didn't know her *yet*.

They weren't privy to the knowledge that phony is what Mariella does best.

I rolled my eyes at Dakota. "Seriously? They haven't even talked since tryouts last year. And last I checked, Mariella and Genevieve hated each other." She nodded, rolling her eyes right back. Mariella was such an attention whore, and leave it to her to use Genevieve's death as a crutch for boosting her own popularity. Honestly, it made me

38

sick.

"You think she had anything to do with it? Do you think she would ki—?"

I slammed my locker door shut, making it bang just loud enough to drown out Sydney's question. "I'll see you next period." I took off jogging, heading toward the same lab as yesterday. Winter was saving me a seat in the back.

"Are you okay?" she asked, looking at me with this pitiful, mom-like expression. I swallowed down a lump of anxiety in my throat, just as Mr. Ellison ordered us to open our chemistry books to page five.

The words blurred together…

I spent the rest of the school day focusing on school for once—if you could call it that—taking rapid fire notes although barely comprehending what my teachers were talking about. On the outside, I looked studious. But inside, I just felt numb.

I still couldn't get over the image of Genevieve's face. Sure, she was sort of a bitch. Well, not sort of—she *was* a bitch. I wasn't like Mariella, pretending to love the girl now that she's dead. But she *was* a fellow squad member, and nobody deserves to go out like that…

I tried to remember every detail. Or tried *not* to but failed, I should say…

The missing flesh from her nose. Her body slumped against the side of the stall, her shiny blonde hair pasted against her odd-colored cheeks.

I remembered something. Blood…there had been blood in her hair, making it a strange orange-ish hue…

Did someone hit her over the head with something?

I squeezed my eyes shut, trying to remember details…details I didn't want to know, but couldn't forget no matter how hard I tried…

She was dressed in gym clothes—a white tank with long boy shorts—which is what she always wore to cheer practice. Blood dripped from her right ear lobe, wiggling its way toward her bare, skinless nose. Genevieve's eyes popped open, two empty black sockets…

"Ahhh!" I startled in my seat, jerking my own eyes open and hastily looking around. I was sitting in French class. Mrs. Rooney stood still at the front, her dry erase marker frozen in mid-air.

Students were staring at me too, a few of them snickering or whispering to themselves.

"She's the one who found the dead cheerleader…"

"Have you heard about her dad…?"

I didn't know if the whispers were real or imagined. Everything seemed surreal, wavy.

"Are you okay?" Mrs. Rooney asked. She was walking toward my desk. When I looked up, I expected her to look angry, but instead she looked…pitying.

"Can I take a bathroom break?" I didn't wait for an answer, just stood up, gathering my backpack and folders.

Moving quickly through the empty hallway, I made a beeline for the girl's bathroom, keeping my eyes on my feet. I counted my steps, determined not to have a panic attack.

I hit a brick wall.

But it wasn't a wall, it was Jordan.

I looked up at him in surprise. Wordlessly, he took my arm, leading me down an empty hallway.

I was too surprised to protest. He urged me inside an empty classroom, closing the door behind him.

I leaned against the teacher's desk, shocked by his rush to get me alone.

"I used to have panic attacks too." He walked over, leaning beside me on the desk. "Is this about Genevieve?" His voice was soft, hesitant.

I took a deep breath then exhaled. "Her and other things. This isn't the first scary incident I've had..."

"Tell me." He said it with such intensity. I stared into his eyes, sensing something so genuine, so safe about him...

"Okay." I nodded and then I started telling him everything. About the sociopath from last year and Sydney's near death experience. I told him about Genevieve, how she looked when I found her...

"If her blood was that fresh, still dripping...then someone couldn't have killed her long before you came in." As soon as he said it, he looked regretful, afraid to set me off again.

"I'm fine now," I assured him. And actually, I kind of was. Talking to him made me feel better.

My heart rate had slowed, my breathing was normal.

Someone must have killed her right after the last class of the day. She changed for cheerleading tryouts and that's when the killer did it. Sometime

41

during the end of the day, shortly before tryouts…

That's when I remembered something.

Brittani Barlow standing by the gym door. Waiting happily, but for what? For who? Why wouldn't she have gone inside the locker room and changed for tryouts? I struggled to remember— what had she been wearing?

Tight jeans and a perky sweater vest, I remembered. Definitely not what she'd wear to tryouts.

Why didn't she go in the locker room to get changed? I wondered. *Maybe because she knew there was a dead girl inside.* My heart raced.

"Tell me what you're thinking right now." Jordan watched me, his expression curious. I wanted to tell him and I *would* tell him, but all I really wanted to do was lean in and kiss him.

He'd been so sweet, so protective of me…

But then the bell rang, interrupting my fantasy kiss.

"Can I walk you to your next class?" Jordan offered, standing up and adjusting his backpack straps. They looked tiny on his broad, tan shoulders.

"Sure." I smiled, the panic I'd felt earlier gone but not forgotten. Somewhere in the back of my mind, I still couldn't help wondering if Brittani was the one who killed Genevieve. She was known to do whatever it took to reduce the competition, including dropping a girl from a stunt last year. That drop resulted in a broken leg that took nearly a year to heal correctly.

Jordan dropped me off at Home Room. "Good luck at tryouts today!" he shouted, smiling so sweetly it made my stomach drop, like the good kind you get when you fall from the peak of a rollercoaster...

And in all of the chaos, I'd nearly forgotten about tryouts...

Chapter Eleven

The Sociopath

Violets are blue.
Roses are red.
Genevieve lost her nose.
Now you'll lose your head…

Chuckling to myself, I tucked the note inside the locker, pleased with my latest poem. What do you know? I can be smart *and* artsy.

If they thought they could get rid of me by sending that moron Ashleigh away, they were *dead* wrong…not only will I eliminate the competition, but I'll cut them up.

One. By. One.

Chapter Twelve

Amanda

Despite my concerns about Brittani's possible guilt, I was still excited about tryouts. This is what I'd been waiting for all summer! Not only was it my chance to be a "veteran" on the cheerleading squad, but it was our first year entering the 2016 All Star Cheer Competition in Dallas, Texas.

Everyone knows it's the most coveted cheer trophy in the country, and I had to make the team so I could get a chance to compete, *and* because I wanted to cheer for Jordan.

Coach Dolly Davis's voice rang out over the intercom, notifying all cheerleading hopefuls that the first day of tryouts would be held outside next to the track.

Because of Genevieve's crime scene, I thought, nervous jitters rushing back to the pit of my stomach.

At the sound of the bell, I made my way outside to the track, eager to run or tumble or practice lifts…anything besides thinking about Genevieve.

The boys' basketball team were running on the track. I immediately recognized Ronnie, Genevieve's boyfriend and my ex, standing with the basketball coach, Coach Purnell, on the sidelines. Unlike Mariella's phony act this morning, it was obvious Ronnie had been up all night last night, and that he'd been crying.

His cheeks were raw and red, and he had ugly bluish-black circles beneath his eyes.

Ronnie's an asshole. He screwed me and Dakota over last year, but at the same time, I couldn't help feeling sorry for him. He obviously had nothing to do with Genevieve's death if he was this distraught over losing her.

A group of girls were clustered in the grassy middle of the track. I made my way toward Dakota and Sydney. They smiled as they saw me coming, waving me over excitedly.

I guess Dakota's not mad at me anymore. That's one good thing, I suppose…

But then a flash of white-blonde hair intersected me. Winter stopped in front of me, slightly breathless and sweaty, but glistening in the way that only a rare breed of girls can do when they're working out.

"Hey, girly!" She jogged in place.

I tried my best to smile back, sneaking a peek at Dakota's sour face behind her.

"Hey, there." I kept walking, heading toward my two best friends.

"I'm so excited, aren't you?" Winter asked, tightening her ponytail as she fell in step beside me.

I had no choice but to lead her straight to Dakota.

I suddenly felt awkward and irritable. *It's not my problem if Winter and Dakota have history. I have enough on my plate without their childish drama.*

I plopped down in the grass, spreading my legs in a V and raising my arms up high above my head to stretch them. Dakota and Winter stared at each other, having their own version of a Mexican standoff.

"Talk to you later," Winter mumbled to me, walking toward a different group of girls.

Dakota smiled, seemingly triumphant. *For what? Being a bitch?* I rolled my eyes, joining my legs together and bending over until my face was touching my kneecaps.

"Did you notice all the new girls?" Sydney plopped down on the ground beside me, leaning back and relaxing in the grass. That girl never stretches. I'll never understand how she doesn't pull a muscle or sprain a leg.

I looked around at the other girls, surprised to realize most were strangers. There were five new girls—probably freshman. Also, I couldn't miss that tangled mess of red hair—Mariella Martin was here, of course.

"Genevieve would have wanted me to fill her shoes. I have to try out, in honor of her memory…" *She was still maintaining that bullshit?*

"Ugh," I muttered, standing up to jog in place.

"Tell me about it. She's such a fake," Dakota snapped, staring at me upside down from where she was bent over in a backbend.

"The *last* thing Genevieve would have wanted

was for her to get a spot on the team," I muttered, noticing a dark-haired freshman girl standing next to Winter. She looked familiar, but she had to be new to Harrow…she definitely wasn't in any of my classes…

Suddenly, the new girl turned, running across the grassy midway. Much to my shock and dismay, she performed a running double full flawlessly.

"What the—?" Dakota dropped from her backbend and stared—as did everyone—surprised to see such a difficult stunt performed by a freshman. By *anyone*, in fact. I don't think I'd ever seen a double full, unless it was on YouTube or TV.

When she finished, the girl casually walked back over, prepping for another tumbling stunt. A few of the new freshmen girls excitedly clapped for her. "Who is she?" I asked, still watching the girl in wonderment.

"That's Lauren," Sydney said, staring at the girl as she performed another flawless tumble—this time a full layout. Her landing was perfect, the technique poised and strong.

"Lauren is in a few of my A.P. classes," Sydney added.

"But isn't she a freshman? I've never seen her before," I mused.

Sydney nodded. "She was supposed to be a freshman, but she's *way* smart. So smart, they let her skip ninth grade. That girl is smart *and* funny. Pretty *and* cute. Not to mention she's dating the hottest new guy in school, Jordan."

"Jordan? Jordan *who*?" I whipped around to look at *my* Jordan, running with the boys on the track.

His eyes were on Lauren, watching her perform a set of perfectly formed toe touches.

Her shoulder length black hair glistened in the sun. *Damn. That girl is hot shit*, I had to admit.

Hearing about her and Jordan made me want to puke on my shoes. Now my stomach felt like it would at the *end* of the rollercoaster ride—nauseous and regretful for riding in the first place...

Now I know why she looks familiar, I thought, remembering the random girl riding home with us after school yesterday. I was so in shock, too confused, and preoccupied to realize she might be his girlfriend...

Thinking a guy like him was single...so stupid of me!

"Yep. *That* Jordan," Dakota chimed in. Was it just me or did she seem to enjoy the fact that I was jealous?

Relieved to see Coach Davis crossing the track, I huddled with the other girls. *Screw Jordan*. I just needed to focus on tryouts. *Especially now that I know how tough my competition will be this year.*

Chapter Thirteen

After respectfully saying a few words to mourn Genevieve, Coach Davis divided us up into teams, having the veterans teach the new girls a group cheer just like we did last year. Only this year, *I* was one of the veterans. Which felt pretty cool, I must admit.

With Genevieve gone—*dead*, I corrected myself—there were only three of us veterans. Me, Dakota, and Sydney. After learning the cheer, Coach Davis announced the girls each of us would be teaching.

I had Mariella Martin—*yuck.* And then I had two perky freshmen—Gabriella and Blakely. The four of us made up a group team. Dakota got stuck with the new superhuman freshman—or sophomore crossbreed and stealer of my new crush, Lauren, as well as one other freshman named Khloe. Sydney got the leftover girls, Libby and Winter.

I set to work, teaching the new girls and Mariella the complicated cheer. First, I demonstrated it for them, and then I taught them one segment at a time.

The routine seemed harder than last year's, with a complicated set of dances moves, a lengthy chant, and then a complicated lift at the end. The hard part would be nailing our standing back tucks at the very beginning of the routine. Gymnastics wasn't my strong suit, and by the looks of the faces of the two freshman girls, it wasn't quite theirs either.

We did three full run-throughs before Dakota wandered over. "My group doesn't need my help. Lauren, the super freak, is making *me* look like the amateur over there…"

Mariella and Blakely lifted Gabriella perfectly, holding her up in the stunt with ease. I was the back spotter, and barely listening to Dakota.

"These freshmen are freakishly good…but at least this year we don't have to worry about Brittani dropping girls from the lifts…" Dakota added.

We did a three count in unison, then performed a fancy cradle toss to lower the teeny tiny freshman Gabriella from the lift. She was cheerful and perky, not to mention a great flier for stunts. Dakota, who was the main flyer last year, seemed to be thinking the same thing I was…this girl could be her replacement. Lauren was only one of many new girls to worry about…

Dakota chewed on her lower lip nervously.

"Let's take a quick break then start back from the top in five minutes," I told the girls, looking around at the other group teams.

Speaking of Brittani…

"Where is she?"

"Where's who?" Dakota asked, picking at a jagged thumbnail. She still looked nervous.

"Brittani, that's who. Why isn't she here?"

Dakota gave me a strange look. "Remember last year? She got cut from the team, silly…"

"I know that! I mean, she's supposed to be trying out today. Apparently, her mom said it was okay to come back. And she was in the gym right before tryouts the other day…right before I found Gen—"

But before I could finish and right on cue, Principal Barlow came sprinting across the school parking lot, straight toward the track and field. Normally prim and poised, she was screaming, her hair wild and voice frantic.

"Help me! Someone! Please God, help me!"

We stared at her in wide-eyed confusion. Only Coach Davis jumped to action, running to meet the principal halfway. Fast, desperate words were exchanged and then Coach took off running inside, followed by Principal Barlow.

Basketball players and cheerleading hopefuls…all of us, took off running behind them.

I didn't know what was going on exactly, but we'd all heard Principal Davis's words to Coach Davis. They were clear as day…

"Her throat has been slit! Someone tried to kill my daughter!"

Chapter Fourteen

I watched from the outer edges of the crowd, my throat constricting and my temples throbbing. Brittani was lifted onto a stretcher by several paramedics. Her mother—Principal Barlow—kept her hands on her daughter's neck, trying to stop the bleeding.

When the gurney was gone, I stared at the pool of blood on the floor. Brittani's eyes were open but who knew if she'd survive. After all, she'd lost *a lot* of blood.

Blood...

I love you, Cookie...that's the last thing my dad said before he took two bullets in the chest. I saw it from the living room window.

Come out with your hands in the air! That's what I heard outside...right before he left.

I'm so sorry, Cookie. He was covered in blood. Spatter on his shirt, sweatpants, and shoes. His neck had these tiny wrinkles, little creases filled with dry blood. And his hands. They were covered the worst.

What did you do, Daddy?

He held me, smearing blood on my chest with his own.

I made mistakes. Huge mistakes. I'm sorry. Just know that I'm sorry, Cookie…

After he was gone…I'd stared down at my hands and Tinkerbell t-shirt, now soaked with a stranger's blood.

And that's when I heard the gunshots and saw my father hit the ground…

I shuddered, body quivering…my mind drifting back to the present—another bloody scene. More horror. *They don't call it Horror High for nothing…*

"Someone attacked her from behind and attempted to cut her damn head off." I don't know who said it; there was a group of freshman boys behind me. I felt like I couldn't breathe again. Coach Davis corralled us all back outside, barking orders as more police sirens rang.

Detective Simms arrived with nearly six other officers.

Probably the entire police force of Harrow Hill, I realized.

"Everyone stay outside!" he barked, causing me to jerk, then stiffen.

Was the psycho who did this still in the building?

Dakota clutched my hand in hers, squeezing it hard. "It's going to be okay," she whispered.

No, it won't. Nothing will be okay. Someone cut off Genevieve's nose. And now someone attempted to slit Brittani's throat!

I wanted to scream those words out at the top of my lungs, waking up all these stupid idiots.

"Guys, come over here, please." It was Coach

Davis talking, using her commanding used-to-be-a-cheerleader pep voice.

"The police are here. We're going to be okay. And Brittani's in good hands. She's probably already getting checked into Harrow Memorial." The basketball coach, who was also Coach Davis's fiancé, was talking to the boys. I could hear him giving a similar speech.

Is this supposed to be a pep talk?

Voices buzzed, like a steady hum of pissed off bees. The way Coach Davis said it, it sounded like Brittani was going into the hospital for a minor checkup.

Someone tried to cut her head off, for Christ's sake!

"Coach Davis, will we still have tryouts tomorrow?"

Without turning around, I knew Mariella was the one asking. "You selfish little bitch," I muttered before I could stop myself. I stared at her, ready to smack her if I had to, but Coach Davis grabbed me by the arm.

"What Amanda is trying to say," she said, giving me a warning glance, "is that tryouts are the last thing you all should be worried about. At this point, we might not even have tryouts this year…"

Wait. What?

As much as I wanted to tackle Mariella for her inconsiderate, ill-timed question, Coach's words felt like daggers in my own chest. *No tryouts…as in, no cheering at all this year?*

I fought the urge to cry. Standing quietly by the doors of the school, we waited for the police to release us. By the time they finally came back out, it was nearly dark outside. I could see Jordan and Lauren in my periphery, holding hands and talking in whispers. Winter caught me looking and frowned. "Are you okay?" she mouthed, looking more concerned than ever. I rolled my eyes.

If one more person asked me if I was okay, I really would smack somebody.

Finally—thankfully—Detective Simms and his deputies said we were being released. They were toting plastic bags of evidence, loading them inside their squad cars.

"All of the basketball players and cheerleaders are accounted for?" Detective Simms asked Coach Purnell.

Coach Purnell nodded.

"Besides Brittani. She was the only one expected for tryouts who didn't turn up today," Coach Davis said, standing next to me.

"Good. Please, everyone call your parents immediately and have them come pick you up. I will be meeting with each of you within the next couple days…for questioning."

"I don't need to call my parents. I have my own car." Ronnie stood with his hands on hips, still looking disheveled and distraught.

"No cars are to leave this parking lot. We are still investigating the scene. This entire school is a crime scene now. So, please have your parents pick you up immediately," Detective Simms repeated, his voice gruff.

"I can't call mine. Neither can Sydney or Dakota. You have our cell phones, remember?" I asked.

The detective nodded, looking exasperated by my question. "You will have your phone back soon enough. In the meantime, I already called all three of your parents. Your mother is picking you up, Amanda."

I groaned, throwing up my hands. I felt disgusted.

For the next hour, I watched other people's parents come and go. Dakota's mother took home Dakota and Sydney. Mariella's stepmom and sister came after that. I even watched Jordan and Winter leave. He waved to me and to his *girlfriend*, climbing in the back of a fancy black sports car.

When Mom finally showed up, I didn't even know it was her. I squinted at a cherry red antique car, surprised to see my mother sitting behind the wheel.

I climbed in tentatively, then stared at her with questioning eyes.

"What'd you do to get this? Rob a bank?"

It was a low blow. Very low, in fact, considering my father did exactly that when he was hard up for cash. His decision cost many people their lives that day at the bank, including a pregnant woman and her eight-year-old son. *It even cost him his own life...*

"You need to apologize." I could feel her glaring at me.

"I'm sorry," I muttered, but I really wasn't. She was as much to blame for me living with Grandma Mimi as my dad was. Unlike him, she was able to take care of me...she just chose not to.

My mom put the ancient car in gear, rolling through the parking lot and out toward the main road.

She spoke up suddenly. "As a matter of fact, this is your grandmother's car. It's been sitting in her garage for ages. It took me a few minutes to get it started."

"Wait. *Grandma's* car?"

I ran my palms across the smooth, faded leather seats. It was nice, a luxury car for someone in the forties or fifties.

"It's from the fifties," my mom said, reading my mind.

"It's hard to imagine Grandma driving this…driving anything or anywhere…"

"Oh, Mimi was quite a showboat in her day. She had money and fame, all of it…she was beautiful and glamorous—quite the charmer, indeed."

"Like my father?" I turned to look at her, really seeing her for the first time since she showed back up in my life. She seemed harder, worn out…but her hands around the wheel were soft, gentle. Images of her tickling behind my ears, pressing her face against mine…the images fluttered in and then they went back out…

"Yes, like your father."

I realized then that she was pulling over, slowing down against a grassy patch on the side of Utica.

"Why are you stopping?" I asked. But she didn't answer—just put the car in park, unbuckled her seatbelt, and turned to look at me.

"Look, I'm not going to make any promises this time…"

Oh boy, here we go again.

"But I love you, Mandy. Always have and always will. You captured my heart the day you were born. You've had my heart ever since. I know my actions don't always match what's inside, but God...I love you, Mandy. I love you so much."

Her eyes brimmed over with tears. Surprisingly, I wanted to hug her.

I realized then how long it'd been since anyone touched me. I saw Mimi every day, but she wasn't like a mother and I didn't have a boyfriend to hold me...*Jordan was the first guy to really hold me and when he pulled me close today, it felt so good...*

But then I remembered his girlfriend, Lauren.

My mother reached across the seat, pulling me in for a hug. I let her hug me, enjoying it more than I'd like to admit.

"Tell me what's going on at school," she said, finally pulling away and looking straight into my face. She looked serious, worried. "Do I need to take you out of that school?"

"Mom, you don't even take me *to* school. How are going to take me out? I don't think you've earned the right to tell me when I can and can't go to high school."

"Okay. You're right. I deserve that. But how can I help? I don't want you to be scared anymore. I might not be good for much, but I'd like to think I'm a good listener. Will you talk to me, honey? Please?"

I looked at my mother, wishing—not for the first time—that she could always act this way, the way she did when she was at her best, sober.

I chewed my bottom lip, thinking about Genevieve and what happened to Brittani.

So, I told her. Everything. About the psychopath last year. About Jordan and his girlfriend. About never fitting in and being odd woman out with Dakota and Sydney. I talked about Genevieve, what it was like when I found her…and I filled her in on the attack against Brittani.

It felt good laying it all out. Letting someone else deal with my problems for once.

***

After that, she took me back to Grandma Mimi's. I expected our "moment" to be over, but instead she ordered pizza and suggested we spend the whole weekend together.

"Having girl time," as she called it.

I felt lost without my iPhone. But there was a part of me—a very prominent part—that felt relieved to be cut off from the world. *Even if I could call someone, who would it be? And did I really want to talk to them?*

No, I decided. Having my mother in the house brought new life to Grandma Mimi too. She dusted off the china, took down three champagne glasses, and put on her favorite black flapper dress.

She and Mom made this seafood Cajun pasta that was unlike anything I'd eaten, with fat peppery jumbo shrimp and creamy pasta with spices I couldn't identify.

I watched the two of them gliding through the kitchen, performing a graceful dance they'd mastered long ago. Mimi isn't my mother's mother, but you couldn't tell it from watching them side by side. It seemed strange to see them mesh so well together. I guess they both loved my father at one point; their failures meshing together, creating some strange, unexpected bond...

The house seemed alive, bluesy music playing—to go with our Cajun feast. I drank wine, a few too many glasses, actually. Mimi never let me drink so I took advantage of this one occasion.

We retired to the living room after dinner, talking about the past. I listened, eager to hear some stories, especially about Vegas.

But the fun was interrupted by sharp rapping at the door.

"Who the hell could that be at this hour?" Grandma Mimi tiptoed to the window, separating the curtains to peer outside.

"Oh. It's that detective."

My heart sank. So much for avoiding the outside world...

Chapter Fifteen

Mom and I sat across from Detective Simms, the only thing between us the table and my cell phone. That and the smell of liquor on my breath. I excused myself, went to the bathroom, and rinsed my mouth with mouthwash as fast as I could.

I sat back down, the bitter aftertaste making my mouth burn.

"We didn't find anything on your phone. No missed calls or texts from unknown numbers. We haven't had any luck tracing the calls from this summer…apparently, whoever is doing this is using a disposable, prepaid phone."

I stared at the phone in question—*my* phone, with its plastic case decorated in tiny, childish stickers.

"Like I said, we haven't heard from anyone in months. After Ashleigh went away to juvie, we each got called a maximum of three times. It was a recording, vague stupid threats about how the cheerleaders would die one by one. We didn't take it seriously…"

Detective Simms waited for me to say more, to fill the awkward space between us.

I rambled on. "I think it was a prankster. Someone trying to perpetuate the drama at Horror— Harrow High, I mean. Or for all we know, it could have been Ashleigh again, calling from inside juvie. They do get some phone calling privileges in there, don't they?"

Mom spoke up. "My daughter should have told you, Mr. Simms. That would have been the responsible thing to do."

I frowned, glaring at my mother angrily.

Who the hell did she think she was? And speaking of responsibility…maybe she should learn how to be a better, more responsible mother.

"Wait. Do you think the person who called them is the same one who killed that girl and tried to kill the other?" my mom asked.

"Their names are Genevieve and Brittani, Mom."

I stared at Detective Simms, wanting to hear his answer.

They both ignored me, talking like I wasn't even there…

"I absolutely do, ma'am," he said.

With that said, Detective Simms placed a Ziploc bag on top of the table. He slid it toward me.

There was a note inside of it, five lines of blood red letters written on the front side of the plain white sheet of paper:

I got murder, yes I do
I got murder, how about you?
We got murder, yes we do

*I'll chop your nose off
And eat it too...*

My heart was pounding so hard I thought it might burst through my chest. I could feel my mother stiffen beside me.

"Who wrote this?" I asked. It was a stupid question. If he knew who wrote it, he wouldn't be sitting here talking to me...

"We found this in Genevieve's backpack. Someone must have sent it to her at some point during the day. Her boyfriend Ronnie said she seemed worried about something at lunch and still seemed upset before she headed to practice. Someone was waiting for her in the girls' locker room. This was premeditated."

"Is that blood?" I pointed at the bright red writing on the note.

"It's being tested, but I don't think so. It's too bright, too fresh."

Detective Simms was watching me, studying my reaction to all of this. He had probably been to see half a dozen other kids from school too, but I couldn't help feeling that he might suspect me because of my family history of violence and craziness...

"That's not all," he said.

I watched in horror as he reached inside his bag, pulling out another note covered in plastic.

I stared at the words, not breathing.

*Violets are blue.
Roses are red.*

Genevieve lost her nose.
Now you'll lose your head...

"In the other girl's locker?" my mom asked, touching the plastic evidence, then pulling her hand back in disgust.

I felt hands on my shoulders from behind. I looked up at Grandma Mimi. She was nervous...more nervous than I'd ever seen her, lips pursed and one eye twitching.

"Will that girl be okay? The one whose throat was—"

"Her name is Brittani,' I interjected, my voice flat.

"I think she'll be fine. She'll have a scar, but that's it. She got lucky. It was a person all in black, face covered, who attacked her in the girl's bathroom. She was getting changed for tryouts, since the locker room and gym were closed. Whoever it was, they were waiting in a bathroom stall. That's according to Brittani's own account."

I shivered.

"A janitor came in and the perpetrator ran. If he hadn't interrupted, I have no doubt Brittani would be dead right now, and this second note—about losing a head—was certainly intended for her."

After showing us the freakish letters, Detective Simms asked me nearly fifty questions. *Did I know of anyone who'd want to hurt Genevieve or Brittani? Anyone who'd want to hurt me? Where did I change for practice? Did I see anyone or anything suspicious? Had I received any notes similar to these notes?*

I can barely recall my answers. Once he was gone, I took my phone and climbed the steps to my bedroom, too mentally exhausted and overwhelmed to do anything.

I crawled beneath the covers, my body still chilled from the creepy words on the notes.

A few minutes later, I heard the door to my bedroom open. My mother kicked her shoes off and climbed in bed beside me. Normally I would have protested, but tonight I was grateful not to be alone.

Chapter Sixteen

I slept till nearly noon on Sunday, too cold to get out of bed and too comfortable to give a damn.

"Ready to eat something?" My mom was sitting on the edge of my bed, making me nostalgic. I turned away from her, squeezing my eyes shut.

When I was little, she and Dad made breakfast every Sunday morning. You wouldn't know it by looking at them, but they never got married.

"I don't need a piece of paper to prove my love," my dad said more than a few times while I was growing up.

"If you love me, don't leave this time."

I don't know where it came from, but there it was—my pathetic plea to be loved.

"I promise. I won't," she said, despite her earlier claim not to make promises.

She sat beside me, wrapping me up in her arms. It felt good, as much as I wanted it not to.

***

School was called off on Monday. And then it was called off Tuesday too. I can't say that I minded. I wasn't ready to go back yet. It poured rain both days, the drizzly, blue-black skies fitting my mood completely. I stayed inside, watching reruns of old corny soaps with my mom and helping Grandma Mimi cook dinner and clean.

My grandma seemed happier than I'd ever seen her, and I couldn't help wondering why—it had to be my mother coming back because nothing else good had happened, that's for sure.

I expected Tuesday to be quiet and calm, but then I got a visitor. It was Coach Davis, and seeing her standing on my front porch dressed in jeans and a frayed t-shirt was strange, to say the least. She seemed so out of her element, less mythical.

"I'm just stopping by to check on you, Amanda. Your cell goes straight to voicemail…" I let her in. We took seats in the living room, both of us feeling awkward.

"I'm totally fine. Eager to get back to tryouts," I lied.

"Good. I don't want to be disrespectful to Genevieve or Brittani, but the show must go on, as the saying goes. I'm going to accelerate tryouts. School is back in session tomorrow. I want everyone to meet after school. We'll practice for an hour and then tryouts will be held. I'll announce the girls who made it on Thursday."

Surprised, I asked, "What about the individual cheer?"

"I think I can make my decision based solely on the group routine. It's not ideal, but it's necessary.

We're already behind. The season will be starting soon and I need cheerleaders on game night."

I nodded. It made sense. "I'll be there tomorrow," I promised. With that, Coach left, using her purse as a shield from the unrelenting downpour.

I stood at the screen door, watching the rain pound the thick black pavement and grass, creating muddy pools all over Grandma Mimi's yard.

Grandma was napping and Mom was in the shower, so I climbed the creaky, twisted staircase and locked myself in my room.

I crawled back into bed, pulling the covers up to my chin. I couldn't get the chill out of my bones. Was it the weather or just the creepy sensation that a killer was on the loose in Harrow Hill?

Sighing, I reached for my cell phone. It'd been sitting on my nightstand—turned off—ever since Detective Simms returned it.

As much as I didn't want to, I turned it on. Instantly, it chimed again and again, an endless reminder of my negligence. Some of the messages and calls were from Sydney and Dakota, no doubt. Plus the usual influx of social media notifications.

I waited for them all to come in then started swiping through each notification, eager to get this over with and take a nap. I had a couple missed calls from Coach Davis and Sydney. I also had a few texts:

Dakota: *Are you okay? I was going to come over but you weren't answering your cell and I thought you might be spending time with your*

mom...

Sydney: Are you okay? Phone going straight to V-mail.

Winter: Hey, girly. I still can't believe what happened. Wow, this new school is turning out to be crazy! Call me if you can/want, please. We can practice the group cheer if you want to...

I felt bad for worrying my friends, but I didn't feel much like talking...even now.

Browsing through my notifications, I saw several new unread emails in my inbox.

One was from an unknown sender. Expecting spam, I opened it. I was met with eight lines of bright red text in the body of the email.

My hands shook. My heart raced. The message read:

Give me an M!
Give me a U!
Give me an R!
Give me a D!
Give me an E!
Give me an R!
What's that spell?!
DEAD CHEERLEADERS.

Chapter Seventeen

This time I did the "responsible thing," according to my mother, by calling Detective Simms right away. He showed up at the door, rain soaked and wide-eyed, eager to confiscate my phone again. He could keep the damn thing for all I cared.

"What about my daughter? She could be in danger!" My mom was standing in the kitchen, her skin white as a ghost.

"I'll have an officer sit outside and keep watch for you tonight. And tomorrow, I'll have several deputies patrolling the hallways and making sure the kids are safe," he said, trying to comfort her.

I should have felt safer, calmer. But honestly, I felt scared to death. I didn't want to end up like Brittani, and I certainly didn't want to wind up dead in a bathroom stall like Genevieve.

Mom slept in bed with me again, but this time I didn't sleep well. I listened to the rain beating against the rooftop, imagining every sound as someone breaking in or creeping down the hallway

71

to get me…

After all, both girls who received notes from "The Prankster" ended up dead or injured shortly thereafter…

I need to stop calling him or her The Prankster because what he/she really is…is a killer.

Chapter Eighteen

I planned to catch a ride to school with Dakota, but Mom insisted on taking me herself despite my endless protesting. There was an officer I'd never seen before parked on the street outside our house. Somehow, his presence there both scared and relieved my inner jitters.

"Maybe you should stay home again," my mom said as she pulled up to park in front of Harrow High.

"I can't hide forever." I smiled at her guiltily. She looked so distressed. I hated making her worry, but at the same time...another part of me felt happy to know she cared so much for once.

I assured her that I would be fine and climbed out.

Eager for a distraction, I made my way down to chemistry lab. We were reviewing the periodic table this week and I was paired up with Winter to quiz each other and practice.

"Are you all right? You never answered my text," she whined when I sat down. She was looking at me worriedly.

"I'm fine. Just spending time with my family." I was tempted to tell her about the frightening email, but decided against it. I didn't want to stir up more drama and terror; that's exactly what the Killer wanted...

In Brit Lit, Sydney and Dakota hovered, continuously asking if I was okay.

"Ready for tryouts today?" Winter whispered. Glad to hear a question that wasn't about me and my well-being, I nodded. I'd nearly forgotten today was the day!

***

The day moved slowly. It seemed like any other day too, except the occasional glimpse of police officers following me and cordoning the hallways. Detective Simms stopped me between classes, returning my cell phone.

"Anything yet?" He shook his head, offering no more information.

When I got to Child Development, I made a beeline for the first table. I didn't want to sit next to Jordan. He'd been sweet and flirty, all while he was dating that girl, Lauren.

And speaking of Lauren...if anyone could screw up my chances of making the team today, it'd be her. Maybe all the missed practice days would make her not do as well...but somehow, that seemed liked wishful thinking. Not only was she dating my super crush, but she was a super freak when it came to doing gymnastics. Coach Davis would be crazy not to let her on the team, as much as I hated to admit that...

I focused on the stages of infant development in the womb, avoiding Jordan's curious gaze from across the room. I nearly sprinted for the door at final bell. Halfway down the hall, I heard Jordan's voice.

"Amanda, please wait!"

I whipped around, trying my best to keep my expression blank.

Don't let him know he hurt you. Don't let him know he hurt you, I repeated over and over in my head.

"What's wrong?" Jordan asked, finally catching up with me.

"Nothing. Why would there be?" I flipped my hair over my shoulder, playing with the loose strings of fabric on my backpack straps.

"Because you're ignoring me. I thought we were friends."

Hearing the word 'friends' set me off.

"You have a *friend*, Jordan. Her name is Lauren. If you'll excuse me, I have to get...to lunch," I recovered, turning back around angrily and walking toward the lunchroom.

"Wait!" he shouted out after me. "I tried to break up with her over the summer, when I thought I was leaving! But since we didn't go, she assumed we were staying together. But the truth is, I really wanted to break up. Not just because we were moving, either..."

I stopped walking, turning around to look at him. His eyes were soft, but troubled.

"Then you should tell her the truth," I said with conviction.

I could literally hear Jordan swallow. "I'm going to. Right after cheer tryouts. I didn't want to upset her and mess up her chances…"

I didn't know what to say. I didn't know how to feel. I really liked him and wanted him to break up with Lauren. But at the same time, I felt sort of bad for the girl. I'd hate to be *that* girl, the one who didn't realize her boyfriend didn't want her…

"I want to be friends. And maybe after…maybe we can be more, Amanda," Jordan said, his lips curling into a hopeful smile.

I couldn't help enjoying the fluttering feeling in my stomach. It wasn't nervousness for once—it was excitement. *Maybe…if he was going to break up with her anyway, then it would be okay for me to see him, right?*

"Okay," I whispered shyly, trying not to blush. We talked all the way to the lunchroom.

Chapter Nineteen

I practically skipped inside the lunchroom, on cloud nine for the first time all year. Jordan headed off to eat with Lauren, smiling apologetically. *Their relationship is just temporary though*, I reminded myself, smiling. I grabbed a spot in line, too happy to eat but knowing I needed to. Selecting a chicken patty, mixed vegetables, a cup of soup, and a bottle of fruit juice, I made my way across the lunchroom.

Dakota, Sydney, and Andy were sitting in their usual spot, but it was Winter who was waving me over from across the room, a big smile on her face.

I hesitated, unsure which direction to go. Finally, I made my way toward Winter. After all, she was sitting alone and she was my soon-to-be-boyfriend's sister.

As soon as I sat down, she pointed. "Look who's back at school!" I turned around just in time to see Brittani Barlow walking slowly with a brown paper sack in her hand. Heavy gauze and tape covered her neck area.

"You can sit with us, Brittani!" Winter shouted,

77

much to my dismay. "Is that okay?" Winter whispered, raising her eyebrows at my wide-eyed expression. I nodded, filling my mouth with chicken and bread.

Brittani sat down slowly, feigning a smile at both of us. She moved like an owl, as though she couldn't turn her neck side to side. I tried not to stare at the heavy bandage, but for some reason, I just couldn't seem to look away.

Brittani, who was normally chipper with a plastered smile on her face, now seemed to wear a new expression. *What was it? Paranoia, maybe?*

Instead of eating, she watched—her eyes darting side to side nervously.

I guess I couldn't blame her after what happened.

"Amanda, quit staring at her!" Winter scolded, eyes wide and warning. Brittani let out a strange giggle, which didn't seem so out of character.

"It's okay, you can look," she said, smiling at me sheepishly. "If it were me, I'd want to look too."

"I'm so sorry, Brittani. We both are," Winter said, eyeballing me with another warning glance.

I cleared my throat. "Yeah, I'm sorry too. I just can't believe someone tried to…to do that to you."

Brittani opened her lunch sack, taking out a sandwich and pear for lunch.

"I can," she suddenly said, looking up at both of us. "And I know who did it."

My mouth fell open just as a loud scream ripped through the air. Winter jumped back, nearly knocking the entire bench over, backing up from me and the table.

She was pointing at me. Well, not me…but my

lunch.

"Y-your s-soup," she pointed, struggling to get the words out. Brittani's expression was flat, but she too, was staring at my bowl of soup.

I looked into the bowl. It was alphabet soup. At first I thought maybe there were freaky words spelled out with the letters. I remembered The Killer's note...*Give me an M! Give me a U...*

But that's when I saw it. The tip of an object poking up through the yellow-ish, murky broth. Using my spoon, I lifted the strange object in the air. Horrified, I dropped it, soup sloshing over the sides and metal hitting linoleum with a loud clanking sound.

It was Genevieve's nose.

Chapter Twenty

More cop cars and sirens. This routine was getting old. *Surely, they've found some sort of evidence by now to catch this person?* I thought, exasperated, staring at a cluster of police officers hovered around the lunchroom table where I'd been sitting.

Students were jammed in the hallway, teachers struggling to keep everyone calm. Finally, Principal Barlow came over the intercom, directing us all to go to the gym.

Like I want to go back to that place, I thought glumly.

"Oh my gosh, I'm so sorry, Amanda." It was Dakota, and she slipped her hand in mine. I expected to feel traumatized all over again, but instead, I was getting pissed. *Who the hell did this person think he was? If the police don't find him soon, I will. And when I do…*

"Amanda, it's time to go! We're all being called to the gym," Dakota whispered, pulling on my hand.

I followed her reluctantly, Andy and Sydney in our wake. "Where's Winter?" I asked, suddenly realizing she was gone.

"Who knows? Who cares?" Dakota muttered, pulled on me harder.

"I'm not in the mood for your jealous drama!" I yanked my hand away, leaving Dakota standing there with her mouth wide open. I fought against the traffic, pushing back through the crowds to look for Winter. She was so freaked out about the discovery in my soup bowl, I just wanted to make sure she was all right...

"Winter!" I shouted, foolishly thinking she could hear through the buzz of hyped up students, all talking about the nose incident.

"I think she did it. After all, her dad's a murderer..." Before I could even tell who said it, I spun around, throwing wild punches.

One of the punches connected with someone's face.

"Oh my god!" someone next to me screamed. A girl lay on the ground, clutching her mouth and nose. My fist did more than connect...I'd really done some damage. Bright red blood oozed between her fingers as she clutched her injured nose.

The girl stared up at me between fingers, horrified. I recognized her as Blakely, one of the freshman girls on my group team. *Shit*.

"See, I told you she's the killer! She's violent! Somebody go get the police!" Blakely screamed from the floor.

Chapter
Twenty-One

Needless to say, I didn't make it to tryouts. Not today. And I wouldn't be at school tomorrow either…

I wouldn't even be at school to hear the girls who made the squad, must less try out for it…

My name would not be on that list.

I was suspended for two days. And worse…Blakely's parents were threatening to sue.

I laid in bed all night, refusing to eat what my mom or grandma brought me, feeling defeated. I let my anger get the best of me and now it had cost me—big time. I wouldn't be cheering for the Harrow Dragons this year, maybe never again…

Finally, I drifted off to sleep at seven-thirty, only to wake back up in the middle of the night. My phone was ringing non-stop, someone calling me back to back…

I looked at the bedside digital clock. It was nearly two in the morning. I'd been asleep for nearly eight hours…

I rolled on my side, staring at the ringing phone.

Can't anyone take a hint? *If I didn't answer earlier, I'm not going to answer now…*

But it kept on, until finally Grandma Mimi knocked on the frame of my bedroom door. The tone of her knock was irritated.

"Either answer the damn thing or turn it off, Amanda!"

Sighing, I picked up the phone and pressed talk. "Hello?"

My question was met with heavy breathing. I sat up in bed, anger rising.

"Listen, asshole! I'm not afraid of you! You're just some stupid copycat! Why don't you get a life, and leave all of us the hell alone?" I screamed into the phone.

Grandma was still at the door, her eyes wide and frightened.

"Don't, Amanda," she mouthed.

"Well, aren't you going to say anything, *prankster*?" I pushed, clutching the phone so tightly my knuckles turned white.

Expecting the robotic voice from before, my back stiffened when I heard the sounds of whimpering coming through the phone.

"Please, someone help me. Please, she's taken me and she's going to kill me…"

It took my brain a few seconds to register the owner of the voice.

But once I did, there was no denying it—the voice belonged to Sydney.

Chapter Twenty-Two

I screamed loud enough to wake the neighbors.

Hours later, I was still hoarse as I sat outside, Dakota huddled next to me while our moms stood out in the yard, speaking in hushed whispers.

Detective Simms had come and gone. He was out there now, looking for my best friend Sydney...

"Are you sure it was her?" Dakota asked. It was the seventh or eighth time I'd heard that question.

Unusually calm, I wrapped my arms around her, rocking her as she cried.

My eyes were dry, all cried out. Part of me felt almost...numb. Too numb to understand the seriousness of this situation...

"I'm sure it was her," I answered drily.

Dakota looked up at me, studying my eyes as though searching for an answer to this mystery.

"I feel like we should be doing something..." Dakota whined.

"Me too, but you heard what Detective Simms

84

said. He's going to check it out, make sure she's okay…"

"But she's not answering her phone!" Dakota cried, holding up her own phone and pointing at its lack of ringing as evidence that the killer actually kidnapped Sydney.

It had to be nearly four in the morning, but every house on the block was lit up. News of a missing girl…

"He's going to find her. She'll be all right," I said.

But my own words rang hollow; I didn't believe them myself. Nothing about this felt right.

We sat side by side, silently wondering what could have happened to Sydney.

Headlights cast tiny bubbles of light on the slick, shiny asphalt of Blackbird Street. A car was coming. I knew before I could even see the car clearly that it was a police car.

"He's back!" Mom eagerly pointed at Detective Simms's cruiser as it slowly pulled up to the driveway.

"Did you find her? Where is she?" I asked, jumping up to my feet and moving closer to his police car. He stepped out, approaching the group of us with an expression that didn't ease my troubled mind.

"She wasn't home. And we can't find her parents, either."

"They're out of town," I said, chewing the inside of my cheek until it felt raw and sore.

"She could be anywhere! Just because she's not there doesn't mean this still isn't all a big joke…"

Dakota protested, her eyes begging Detective Simms to agree with her.

"There were signs of struggle in the house, like Sydney tried to fight back against her kidnapper."

I gasped, reality sinking in. This wasn't a joke, some stunt performed by a *prankster* to get our attention…

The same person who killed Genevieve and tried to kill Brittani had now taken my best friend.

Chapter
Twenty-Three

I was still in bed when my phone rang well after noon. Despite all that had happened, my mind and body felt exhausted, probably due to the stress. I clenched my teeth, afraid of what I'd hear on the other end...I was relieved when I heard the sound of Dakota's voice.

"I'm calling from the girl's bathroom between classes. Just wanted to tell you that because of Sydney's disappearance, Genevieve's murder, Brittani's attempted murder, and your suspension...Coach Davis has called off cheerleading tryouts again. She said she can't make a decision in lieu of recent events, and cheerleading has been called off...indefinitely."

I sat up in bed. "The last thing I care about is cheerleading, Dakota!" I hissed. "Our best friend was kidnapped. And she might dead!"

Dakota sat quiet on the other end. "I don't care either, honestly. I just wanted to talk to someone.

I'm so scared and worried about Sydney…"

I instantly regretted losing my temper. "I'm sorry for snapping at you. Do you want to come over after school? We need to talk about this and make a game plan. If those cops can't solve this thing, we might need to do it our damn selves. I'm getting my friend back, one way or another."

"I hope so…" Dakota whimpered. I reminded her again to come over after school and then hung up.

Climbing out of bed, I started making my way downstairs, expecting smells of breakfast where there were none. Where was my mom and Grandma Mimi? They'd been so lively these last few days that the house seemed quiet and strange.

I immediately felt concerned. Grandma's bedroom was on the bottom floor, and I stood at her door, listening.

Soft moaning sounds were coming through the thick sliding doors to her room. I pounded my palms against the doors, shouting her name, panicked.

"Come in," Grandma Mimi moaned. She was lying on her side in bed, her face contorted in pain. I ran to her side, fear surging through every vein in my body.

"What's wrong?" I asked, squatting down beside her bed.

"I just don't feel well, is all," she said, barely opening her eyes to look at me. "I'm having growing pains," she added, laughter turning into a whooping cough.

"Should I take you to the doctor, Grandma?"

She shook her head, rolling away from me to her other side.

"No, sweet baby. Just let me sleep a little longer, please. Your mother is here. Have her make you breakfast…or lunch, at this hour…"

I pressed my hand against her forehead, expecting her to feel feverish. Instead, she felt cool and clammy.

"Can I bring you anything?"

"No, baby. Just let your grandmother rest…"

I backed away, finally relenting and returning to the living room.

"Where's Mom?" I wondered out loud, roaming the shadowy hallways of Grandma Mimi's house.

I quickly found my answer. The door to the guest bedroom was closed, but it had been left unlocked. My mom was lying under the covers, her pale moon-shaped face pressed against a down-filled pillow. I edged closer, staring at her face. We sort of looked alike from this angle…

"Mom, are you okay?" I whispered, wondering if maybe she and Mimi were coming down with the same flu bug.

But when I tried to lift the covers, I saw the belt around her arm. Hurriedly, I pressed my finger to her neck, feeling for a pulse. She didn't budge when I touched her or said her name, but her pulse was steady, practically normal.

I pulled the covers all the way down, staring at the purplish bruise on her inner elbow. She had passed out while shooting up. It wasn't the first time this had happened, and surely wouldn't be the last.

I wanted to scream and yell, but somehow…I

didn't have it in me. She'd hurt me so much, that my disappointment meter hit its threshold a few years ago. I sat on the edge of her bed, staring at this person who I loved so much but who always disappointed me.

Finally, I pulled the covers back up to her chin and left, roaming the streets of Harrow Hill all alone. *What did it matter if the killer got me? My life sucked anyway...*

Chapter Twenty-Four

The Sociopath

It's amazing how many idiots walk home from school each day. If they only knew I was watching…imagining what it feels like to gut them in the middle of the street in broad daylight…

The trees behind the track and field were gnarly and tall…great trees for hiding behind.

I waited forever, hours it seemed, for the school building and parking lot to empty out. Once clear, I made my way in through a side entrance and padded down the empty hallways, looking for locker number thirty-nine.

I turned the dial three times, then lifted the latch. It was filled with neatly stacked books. I propped my note on the top shelf, then left my present on top of the note.

Closing the locker, I slipped out through the way I came in…all the while reciting the chant I knew they'd love…

United we stand
Divided we fall
The sound of Sydney's screaming
Just made my skin crawl

Chapter Twenty-Five

Amanda

"Where the hell have you been?" my mother demanded as I slipped back inside the front door. I was sweating and breathless from my long walk up and down the streets of Harrow Hill. I felt better, less angry. The air was cold for September and the chill had cleansed me.

That was until I saw Detective Simms sitting at my kitchen table again.

He turned around, eyeing my disheveled clothes and haggard appearance suspiciously. "I went for a walk," I said, my breath catching in my throat.

"Have you heard from Sydney?" the detective asked.

"No. If I'd heard from Sydney I would have called you. Why are you here instead of out there looking for her?" I demanded, my voice louder than I'd intended.

My mom was quick to defend him. "*I* called him. I woke up from a nap and you were gone. I was terrified that someone took you too. You know better than to leave without telling me! And you shouldn't be out walking alone!"

"I'm sorry, Mother. Next time, I'll use *your* judgment." I said it slow and with bitterness, hoping she'd take the hint. I stared at the now-covered sore on her arm. She caught me looking and crossed her arms over her chest.

"I'm just glad you're okay," she said, her voice softening.

I looked away from her, focusing on Detective Simms. "Has anyone heard from Sydney's parents?"

"That's the thing…we can't find a contact number for them and we've tried everything. They might be out of the country. I was hoping you might know more…" Detective Simms waited, looking at me expectantly.

I sat down in the chair opposite of him.

"The only thing I know about them is that they work in stocks and Sydney said they were out of town. Her dad drives a silver Mercedes and he picks her up from practice sometimes. Dakota should know more. She and Sydney are closer than Sydney and I…"

"And why is that? Were you and Sydney fighting about something?" he asked.

I couldn't help it—I groaned. These questions were just ridiculous! Not to mention downright pointless and a waste of time.

"Of course not," I snapped. "It's just…I only

moved here last year, and she and Dakota have been friends since they were little."

Detective Simms nodded, seeming to accept my answer. Leaning forward, he reached toward my hair, removing small bits of crunched up leaves.

"What were you doing in the woods?"

"I wasn't in the woods. Well, I *did* stop near them...to tie my shoe and look around. There's a killer running around out there; I was hoping I might run into him. 'Cause God knows you're not out there catching the killer..."

"You don't *actually* suspect my daughter of being involved in anything, do you?" My mom's face had gone from worried to terrified. I noticed she was scratching at her arms, right around the injection site. *Probably thinking about her next fix*, I realized angrily.

"No, we don't suspect your daughter. But sometimes I have to ask hard questions to get very simple answers. I'm sure we'll find Sydney soon, but any lead I can get might help the outcome of the investigation."

His answer came as a relief to me, although I tried not to let my face show it. The last thing I needed was for him to suspect me of hurting my friend. Detective Simms stood up, slipping a light windbreaker jacket over his bulging arms. He had to be almost fifty, but his body was fit and toned, making him look much younger.

"What can I do to help Sydney? I feel so worthless at this point. Her phone goes straight to voicemail and she's not home. I don't know where to look or who to call," I moaned.

"The best thing for you to do is go to school and go home, but that's it. Don't go anywhere by yourself. And don't get in any more fights at school." He shot me a warning glance.

"What you *can* do is call any family or friends of Sydney's that you know of. Check out her online friends. If you see someone I should talk to, write down their name and call me. We'll do everything we can to find her. I'm going to make a visit next door and see what I can find out from Dakota."

Despite his cold questions earlier, his face seemed softer now. I nodded. "I absolutely will. I'll call right away if I think of something or someone you need to talk to."

I watched him leave through the door then turn left, heading for Dakota's house next door. I hoped and prayed she had more information to offer than I did. Anything that could help find Sydney…

I tried to imagine never seeing her again. We weren't as close as Dakota and I, but we'd had so much fun the other night, hanging out and having a sleepover.

Tears stung my eyes and my mother rushed over, eager to comfort me.

"Don't touch me!" I said, jerking away from her angrily.

She stared at me, shocked. "What did I do? I'm just trying to help!"

"I know you're using again, Mom."

Expecting her to deny it, I shot her a hard stare, like a mother waiting for an explanation from a child.

My mother exhaled. "I'm sorry, honey."

She wrapped her arms around me anyway, and I didn't push her off this time. At least she hadn't denied it—that seemed like a step, albeit a baby one...

Chapter Twenty-Six

Sydney's chair sat empty beside me, a constant reminder that she wasn't at school and nobody knew when she was coming back. *No one even knows where the hell she is, in the first place...*I had a sudden thought—*what if her parents came and got her, took her away for a while because of all the crazy incidents that happened last week?*

But she still would have called and told us—me and Dakota, at the very least...

Brit Lit seemed less crowded and quieter today. I looked around, expecting to find more students absent but the only one missing was Sydney.

Maybe it was just a somber cloud hovering above the students at Harrow Hill. We were all afraid of what might happen next...

When the bell rang, I caught up with Dakota. Winter, in turn, caught up with me—and the next thing I knew, all three of us were walking together.

Dakota and Winter didn't talk or look at each

other. I'd become the proverbial monkey in the middle, not knowing who to talk to or how to bridge the gap between them.

"Did Detective Simms come to either of your houses last night?" I directed the question to both of them, looking from one to the other as we made our way through a long line of band members, some of their instruments bumping my hips as we passed them.

"He did. I didn't have much to say that could help him, but I tried to answer everything honestly. I gave him the cell numbers I have for Sydney's parents...I'm sure they'll be devastated when they find out," Dakota said.

"Maybe they should blame themselves, while they're at it. What kind of parents leave their child alone for that long?" Winter demanded.

I felt like saying, *At least Sydney's parents aren't dead or a junkie like mine, but I bit my tongue, focusing ahead on my locker.*

"Well, they work in stocks and Sydney is reliable. If she were my daughter, I'd trust her!" Dakota said defensively.

Here we go...I imagined a bell ringing, like round one in a boxing match. These two *really* didn't like each other.

"Look, I'm sorry for insulting your friend's parents, but that's just crazy for her to be alone like that," Winter softly said.

That's when I remembered—Sydney had a grandmother named Rose. I'd never met Rose, but I struggled to remember what she was like and what her full name was. Sydney talked about her on occasion…*where did she live again?*

"Do you remember Sydney's grandma?" I asked Dakota, ignoring Winter's speech.

Dakota furrowed her eyebrows, thinking. "I think so. But doesn't she live in Tulsa?"

"Hmmm. I don't remember. But maybe that's who we should call."

"Most people aren't listed in the phone book these days. I wonder how easily we can find her," Dakota mumbled.

"Facebook. Everyone and their *grandma* has a Facebook profile these days," Winter chimed in.

I smiled, pleased with this new idea. But then I remembered that tracking down Grandma Rose wouldn't get me any closer to finding this freak who took Sydney.

But at least someone in her family could be reached until Detective Simms reached her parents. Somebody needed to be notified.

***

I collected makeup assignments from my teachers, looking away in embarrassment as they gave me scolding looks for my recent suspension. Apparently, everyone knew about me punching that loudmouth, Blakely.

Relieved to see Jordan, I plopped down at our table in Child Development, leaning close to him.

"I'm so glad you're back," he whispered into my hair. "I was so worried about you. Has anyone heard from Sydney?"

I shook my head, trying to fight back tears again.

I was starting to feel like an emotional train wreck. Jordan saw the tears coming and pulled me in for a hug.

"That'll be enough of that! If you want to practice being a grownup, you can start by taking one of these." Mrs. Brooch dropped an enormous cardboard box on our table, making the entire table wobble and shake. I leaned forward in my seat, peeking over the side of the box.

It was filled with life-like baby dolls. "Creepy," I said, leaning back in my chair.

"Jordan and Amanda, perhaps the two of you would like to share a baby. Then you can get a true sense of what it feels like to be an adult couple."

I looked over at Jordan sheepishly. "Absolutely, Mrs. Brooch. We'd love to." He reached inside the box, pulling out a baby doll by its foot. The baby immediately began crying, a high-pitched shrill sort of scream.

"Oh, lucky you. You picked the addicted baby," Mrs. Brooch said with a smile. "She needs extra special attention."

I groaned.

Chapter Twenty-Seven

After instructing us on how to properly hold, change, and feed our babies, Mrs. Brooch sent us to our next class with one warning: she could monitor the quality of care we were giving our baby through hourly email reports and those reports would be used to grade us as parents accordingly.

The baby was heavier than I'd expected, weighing at least seven pounds—to mimic the weight of a *real* baby, I presumed.

It cried as we walked down the hallway. I stopped in the middle, disregarding annoyed students behind me, and dug around in the pack Mrs. Brooch gave us for the baby bottle. I pressed the bottle to the baby's lips, simulating feeding as I made my way to my locker. Other students from my class were doing the same thing, or else I would have felt quite foolish.

"Can you hold Annie?" I asked, handing her off to Jordan as I reached my locker.

Getting it open one-handed would be impossible. I had a feeling lots of simple tasks were going to be difficult with this stupid fake baby in tow.

"Sure. Her name is Annie?" Jordan laughed, leaning against the locker beside me and coddling the baby in his arms.

I smiled at him goofily. "Is that name okay with you?" I teased.

He rocked and fed our baby, looking like a natural.

After that, we made our way to the lunchroom, switching off while the other stood in line to get their lunch. I let him go first and by the time I got back to our table with my tray, the forty-five minute lunch period was almost over and Baby Annie was lying on the bench next to Jordan, while he chatted with some of his new basketball teammates. Sighing, I took the baby in one arm, scarfing down a grilled cheese sandwich with the other just as the bell rang for next period.

***

The baby cried off and on all day. I bounced it on my lap and rocked it side to side—avoiding the smirks of my classmates—but all the same, the damn thing still cried. I used it as an excuse to take more than a few bathroom breaks.

Perched on a skinny bench in the bathroom, I stared at the bright blue eyes and waxy skin of the doll. "If you were mine and Jordan's baby...you'd be much cuter," I mumbled.

By the end of the day, I was so worn out I'd

barely thought about the psychokiller or cheerleading or my missing friend...perhaps this baby would be a welcome distraction for the next few days.

I tried to find Jordan at the end of the day, to see if he'd take Baby Annie home with him. I figured switching off each day would probably be the easiest—and fairest—way for us to help each other ace the project.

But I didn't see him near his locker and his car wasn't in the school parking lot. Sighing, I climbed into the back of Dakota's convertible, strapping the baby in tight beside me.

"Aren't babies supposed to use a car seat?" Andy looked over the shoulder of the passenger seat, flashing that joker smile of his. I rolled my eyes, fighting the urge to smack him.

"Good luck with that thing," Dakota said, eager to drop me off once she pulled up out front. The baby had cried the whole way home, even when I tried to change and feed it...

Luckily, my mother was home and I pawned the baby off on her. "Just while I take a power nap..." I pleaded.

Thankfully, she let me sleep for a few hours. When I got up, I remembered Sydney's Grandma Rose. I pulled up Facebook on my phone and clicked on Sydney's profile. She had nearly two hundred friends, and I began the very slow and painful process of scanning the names and profile pics of each.

"What are you doing?" my mom asked, standing in the doorway of my room, rocking Baby Annie in her arms. She looked…motherly, for once.

"Looking for anyone related to Sydney. Detective Simms said they still haven't reached her parents."

"Well, isn't she friends with her parents on Facebook?" Mom asked.

I rolled my eyes. "No one is friends with their parents on Facebook. Unless they're forced to be." I specifically remembered Sydney saying she wasn't Facebook friends with her mom or dad; in fact, she'd said they weren't even on Facebook and didn't understand what it was about…

But after a few more minutes of scanning, I got lucky when I found Rose Cartwright. I wasn't sure if it was her mom's mom or her dad's mom, but either way—this had to be the lady.

She was a tiny old lady with bright rosy cheeks and professionally curled hair. This had to be the Grandma Rose Sydney was always talking about…and I felt pretty sure I'd seen her picture in one of Sydney's framed photos at her house.

I sent this Rose person a friend request and then messaged her:

Me: Hi, there. I'm Sydney's friend, Amanda. I can't get in touch with her parents to let them know Sydney is missing. Have you heard from her? Do you know how to reach her parents? Please message me back and let me know. This is important.

I stared at the message, reading over it again and again, then finally clicking send. I stared at the tiny messenger bubble, hoping she'd read it right away. Apparently, she wasn't online right now.

I arrowed back to Sydney's profile and clicked on one of her albums. Pictures of her in her cheerleading uniform, group pics of all of us, and silly memes filled the album. I stared at my friend's face, willing her big saucer eyes to give me a hint. *Where the hell are you, Sydney? And most importantly,* who *took you?*

The baby was crying again. I looked over at my mom, who I'd almost forgot was sitting next to me on the bed. She rocked the tiny artificial infant, staring at me all the while.

"I've seen these things before. These "think it over" babies, or whatever they're called…but I've never seen one that cries this much. Why does your baby cry so much?" she asked, rocking it harder to make it stop.

"Because her mother was a drug addict." It came out sharp and mean, but I guess in truth, that's how I'd intended it to sound.

My mom stared at me, wild-eyed. "They gave you an addicted baby? What does that mean?"

I sighed, staring back down at my phone. No new Facebook messages…

"It means Mrs. Brooch hates my guts, so she set it on a more difficult setting. My baby has special needs, and it cries…a lot."

"I have a feeling it's going to be crying through the night…" Mom pondered.

I groaned, feeling exhausted just thinking about it.

"Want me to keep it in my room?" she offered.

I shook my head. "I don't need your help. I can handle things on my own." It had a double meaning, and she gave me a hurt look.

Leaning forward, she kissed me on the forehead. "For what it's worth, I love you." She handed me the baby doll.

I checked my messages one last time, then curled up on my bed, cradling my newborn baby.

Chapter Twenty-Eight

I pressed the pedal down, accelerating through the eerily vacant streets of Harrow Hill.

The old car stalled at fifty, refusing to go any faster.

My eyes burned, due to lack of sleep and the freezing cold wind that burned my face. I drove with the windows down.

Despite the chill and my sleepiness, I felt angry and free. I turned the volume up on the radio when I heard Adele's voice pouring out. The radio crackled with static, but I belted out the lyrics to her saddest song as I charged through the streets of this horrible town.

I shouldn't be driving. Not while I was this tired. Not this late at night. And especially since I didn't have my driver's license…

Releasing my lead foot from the pedal, I slowed down as I passed through Crimson County.

I was getting closer to my destination.

My eyes drooped but I fought against it—the overwhelming desire to just close my eyes and let go of everything—all the anxiety and pain.

But then I saw the cemetery gates glistening ahead in the moonlight.

It used to be a town called Flocksdale. Bad things happened here. *Did the evil seep into Harrow Hill?* I wondered, parking the car in front of the gate.

There were no houses for miles, only businesses lining the sullen streets, all closed down for the day.

The cemetery was dark and empty, sitting on a small hill by itself. The gates were locked tight every night as expected, but I knew how to get inside. I left the car running, pausing momentarily to look at the baby. Decidedly, I left Annie lying on the seat—jogging all the way around the property, moving for what seemed like miles.

Where the gate ended was the beginning of a dark wooded area, grass and brush so tall and thick no would be stupid enough to try to venture in.

But this wasn't the first time I'd been here.

I pushed my way through the gnarly branches, the only light guiding me was the moon—a tiny sliver of it poking through the canopy of leaves above me.

I stumbled past trees and overturned branches, careful not to fall and get hurt, or get hung up on any sharp branches.

Finally, I made it through, breaking into the back of the still cemetery.

Hundreds of rows of tiny graves. This is where my father was buried.

I'd only been here a few times, but I remembered just where it was.

The second row from the back—that's where they'd buried my father.

Moments later I was standing in front of it, hands awkwardly clasped behind my back. *Why in the hell did I come here?*

Terrance Loxx's grave was small, probably the cheapest stone money could buy.

His name was on the tombstone, along with tiny dates for his birth and death below it. No dedications, no words to mark his life or who would miss him...

They put him in the back for a reason. This is where the bad guys belong, hidden from the world, pushed to the back in hopes that people will forget.

I kneeled down in front of his grave.

"I hate you," I said.

I willed myself to cry but couldn't.

"I hate you," I repeated, my voice louder as it caught in the wind and floated out of the graveyard.

Reaching out, I traced the name on his grave with my fingers.

"I know I have all of these good memories of you, but the bad ones cancel them out. I *want* to miss you. I *want* to love you. I want to forgive you for what you did."

But I can't.

I sat there, still as a tombstone myself, waiting for something to happen. *A change of heart, perhaps?*

But one never came.

Finally, I went back out the way I'd snuck in,

sliding back behind the wheel. I had to get back home, before mom or Grandma Mimi realized I was gone—along with Grandma Mimi's car.

So much for making amends with my father...

Chapter
Twenty-Nine

"Take this baby."

Jordan was leaning against his locker—Lauren by his side, I noted—chatting with a group of basketball players about their upcoming opponent, the Tugglesworth Tigers. I flinched, remembering that there probably wouldn't be any cheerleaders on game night, due to our once again postponed tryouts. The only good thing about it getting pushed back is that I didn't miss the opportunity to go while I was suspended...

"Take this baby," I repeated, my voice getting louder. Jordan took one look at my wrinkly outfit and flat, tangled hair and he laughed.

"Late night?" he teased, poking me in the belly.

"Looks like your baby needs a daddy," one of the boys joked, nudging the boys beside him and Jordan.

Jordan's face reddened; clearly he was embarrassed. Lauren, who was standing in his

112

shadow, gave me an apologetic smile.

"I have a test this morning. I'll take it at the end of the day and keep it tonight," Jordan mumbled.

"*Its* name is Annie," I reminded him before walking off, instantly feeling silly and overly sensitive.

"Your brother is sort of being a jerk," I said, stopping at Winter's locker. She was taking out her chemistry book, getting ready for our first period class.

Winter sighed. "Look, Amanda, I love my brother to death. But, seriously? He's not *sort of* a jerk. He *is* a jerk. Especially when it comes to his girlfriends."

This was news to me. "Yeah, I heard about him and Lauren getting ready to split up. But I thought me and him had something good going on..."

Before I could finish that thought, a stack of Winter's textbooks fell to the ground. Jumping back, I barely missed getting some pretty sore toes.

Winter was staring at a box on the floor. There was a note stuck to the bottom of it, written in tiny, blood red letters.

"Not again," I hissed, looking around the hallway. *What was I looking for?*

"Someone go get Principal Barlow, now!" I shouted to no one in particular. Students started gathering around to see what was going on.

"Don't touch—" I started to say to Winter, but it was too late. She had picked up the note and box.

Leery, I peered over her shoulder, quickly reading the killer's words:

United we stand
Divided we fall
The sound of Sydney's screaming
Just made my skin crawl

At the sight of Sydney's name, my entire body flinched. "What's in that box?" I asked, my voice sounding weird and tinny—not like my own.

Sliding the top off slowly like someone who was getting ready to receive a diamond bracelet or necklace of sorts, Winter peeked inside...

She let out a blood-curdling scream. She jerked, jarring the box. It fell from her hands, hit the floor, and bounced.

I stared at something slimy and pink on the floor, my brain barely able to register what it was...

It was somebody's tongue.

Chapter Thirty

I rode home from school in a daze, barely hearing my mother's words of encouragement. "It will okay," she said, or something stupid to that effect.

Could someone survive without a tongue?

And without a tongue...would they even want to?

Was my friend dead?

I pictured Sydney's long, silky black hair falling around her face and mouth. She wasn't the type to make jokes. She was serious, sometimes intense, and even a little narcissistic. But I'd grown quite fond of her since last year, and the thought of never seeing her again...that some crazy psycho had cut out her tongue...it was all too much for me to bear. Certainly too much for me to wrap my brain around.

Please, let this all be some sort of sick joke...

I'd passed off the plastic baby to Winter, demanding she give it to her brother for the night. As soon as my mom pulled up, I jumped out and ran inside Grandma Mimi's house. Closing myself in the bathroom, I turned the faucet to the bathtub on

115

and got the water hot enough to burn the memories away.

I waited till the water was close to the brim, then climbed in, water splashing over the side and drenching the tiled floor.

I didn't care. I needed to feel clean, free from that disgusting tongue, even though I hadn't touched it.

There was a knock at the door. "Dakota keeps calling, honey, and she just stopped by too. She's upset and really wants to talk to you," my mom said, her mouth pressed up to the door.

"Not now," I said, slipping beneath the water. Opening my eyes, I stared up through the wavy surface, thick bubbles burning my eyes. *Please God, don't let my friend be dead...*

I stayed in the tub until the water turned cold, then I got out and put my same clothes back on. Moments later, my mom was knocking again, reminding me that we had to attend Genevieve's funeral service at Merschel's Funeral Home. I'd nearly forgotten, and a funeral was the last thing I wanted to go to...

It suddenly dawned on me that I might be attending my best friend's funeral soon too.

***

Despite what happened at school today, the service for Genevieve was packed. So packed indeed, that people had to wait for a turn to go inside the viewing room. I stood next to my mom, waiting behind and in front of clusters of kids, all from Horror High.

It sure earned its name this time, I thought glumly.

"I heard the cause of death was blunt force trauma. Someone hit her over the head with something."

I shuddered, not bothering to turn around. I recognized the voices of some of the freshmen, one in particular—Blakely.

No more punching people, I reminded myself.

If my mom knew the girl behind us was Blakely, she probably would have made me apologize.

I'm not sorry, I realized.

Finally reaching the room with Genevieve's casket inside it, I heard another freshman girl asking, "Did they sew her nose back on?"

What the hell was wrong with these people? I mean, I couldn't stand Genevieve, but still...have a little respect, people!

My mom must have heard it too because she reached for my hand, squeezing it gently and nodding. We moved ahead, finally getting our turn to go up to the casket.

It was closed, and I couldn't help feeling grateful. Images of her butchered face and slumped body would be forever engraved on the backs of my eyelids.

Framed photographs of Genevieve lined the casket. She was so pretty, with her silky blonde hair and aristocratic nose. I wanted to remember her like that—the way she looked in the photos, not the way she looked slumped over that toilet seat...

The coffin itself was beautiful, trimmed in gold

with delicate rose carvings. I stole a glance in the direction of her parents. I'd seen her mother and father at plenty of basketball games. They were always the ones standing up and cheering, getting too worked up over a high school game.

But today they were quiet and sullen, of course. I couldn't even begin to imagine how they felt…

Mom and I hung around for a few more minutes, then made our way back outside.

As soon as we were in the car, something broke inside me. I slumped across the seat, reaching for my mom. "Oh, please don't let Sydney be dead…" I begged, crying against her chest.

She rubbed my hair and held me, then took me out to get some ice cream. It didn't make me feel better, but I did stop crying.

When we got home, I crawled into bed again—my new favorite spot—wishing all of this could be some awful nightmare I'd wake up from, and my life would just be normal again…or as normal as it could get for me, that is…

Chapter
Thirty-One

A soft rapping sound at the door woke me up. *What time is it?* I wondered, stiffening in bed.

Soft moonlight beamed through the curtains. My clock read 11:36 p.m.

The light knocking sounded again. It wasn't coming from my bedroom door but rather, downstairs. Someone was at my front door.

It seemed so strange for a school night, but thinking it might be news about Sydney, I shoved the covers aside and padded down the stairs as quickly as possible without slipping in the dark.

Grandma Mimi might be up—she often stayed up late and sometimes woke me up with her bizarre singing—but I could hear sounds of Mom's soft snoring coming from her room downstairs and the lights were off in Grandma Mimi's room.

I approached the front door, hesitant. *What if the killer is at the door?*

But it seemed unlikely a killer would simply

knock this late on a school night. I peered through the side pane, surprised to see Winter standing on my porch. She was dressed in a light yellow jacket, her black eyes smudged with day-old eyeliner, her hair tossed up in a careless bun.

"What are you doing here?" I whispered, quietly opening the door. She slipped inside, looking embarrassed.

"Can I sleep at your house? I can't sleep, what with that annoying baby over there, not to mention what happened today. I keep thinking the killer is going to show up and kill me. Take my tongue too!"

I made a pained face, remembering Sydney...

"Sorry," Winter added, suddenly realizing it was my friend's tongue she was so brashly speaking about.

"Come upstairs, just be quiet so we don't wake up my mom and grandma," I warned, leading her up the stairs to my bedroom. I turned the light on, closing the bedroom door behind us.

"Are you okay? I'm sorry I just took off. I know you're the one who found her—*it*, in your locker. But I was so freaked out myself, I had to get out of there..." she said, apologetically.

"It's okay, really."

Winter smiled at me, plopping down on my unmade bed, looking around at my posters.

"I wonder if they found any clues in Sydney's bedroom," she wondered aloud.

I sat down on the bed too, picturing Sydney's room and how it looked so neat and clean when I stayed the other night.

"We should go over there. See if she left any

clues," I said. It was so random of me to say, and the idea completely surprised me. *Where did that come from?*

Winter's eyes lit up, like this would be an adventure. "I have my brother's car. We could drive over there, if you think we can get inside."

"We can figure it out or…" I thought for a minute, about how long Dakota and Sydney had been friends. "If there's an extra key hidden outside somewhere, like under a rock or planter, Dakota would know about it. We should ask her to come along."

The thought of actually going inside Sydney's empty house should have frightened me, but for some reason, I didn't care. I wanted to find out who took my friend and I was willing to take some risks to do it.

I pulled out my cell phone, dialing Dakota's number. As it rang, I peered out my side window, checking to see if her bedroom lights were on next door.

Her bedroom was dark. I tried a couple more times, then resorted to texting her.

Me: Are you up? Late night mission: we need you.

I stared at the 'we' part. Usually 'we' meant me and Sydney when I was texting Dakota, but now Sydney was gone…

"I still have feelings for Andy."

I whipped around, staring at this white-haired stranger on my bed. *Really? Of all the times to confess her feelings for my best friend's boyfriend,* now *is the time she does it?*

Fighting the urge to smack her, I found my Keds and slipped them on, then I opened my closet to get a jacket out.

"I'm going to forget you told me that for now, 'cause we're going over to Dakota's to wake her up. Tonight—my only focus is figuring out something that can help us find Sydney."

Chapter
Thirty-Two

It wasn't my first time throwing rocks at Dakota's window, and like the last time, she poked her head through the curtains after a few minutes. She met us outside moments later.

"Get in," I said, pointing at Jordan's Mazda parked in the street.

"I'm not going anywhere with her." Dakota was sleepy-eyed and groggy, but her focus was clear—she still hated Winter and didn't trust her one bit.

Can't say I really blamed her after learning she was still after Andy...

"Listen, Dakota. I'm sorry for kissing Andy last year. I didn't know you guys were seeing each other...and the truth is, well...Andy and I have known each other since we were kids. We'll always have feelings for each other," Winter explained.

If looks could kill, Winter would already be dead. Dakota glared at her. For a moment I was worried she might be the one throwing punches today…

"Nope. Still not going," Dakota said, shaking her head back and forth childishly.

"Do it for Sydney," I pressed, walking toward the car and leaving them both behind.

Moments later, Dakota climbed in the back and Winter took the driver's seat. "I don't know where she lives," Winter said, starting up the engine and pulling away from the curb as quietly as possible.

"I don't know where she lives," Dakota mocked in the back.

"Shut up, both of you. I'll give you directions," I ordered.

Less than five minutes later, we were parked in front of Sydney's hulking McMansion.

"Nice house." Winter stared up at it, suddenly looking frightened. "Are you sure no one's home?" she asked, voice quivering.

"For Sydney's sake, let's hope there is. I haven't been able to get a hold of her grandmother and Detective Simms can't seem to reach her parents," I murmured.

The house was dark. I felt overwhelmed by a feeling, something inexplicable—dark and ominous.

Dakota got out behind me and Winter came around from the driver's side. We stood in Sydney's driveway, unsure what to do now.

"There's a key in the back, in one of those extremely fake looking rocks," Dakota told us. We cut through the yard and circled around to the back of the house. It was eerily quiet outside, albeit the usual songs of summer around here—a chorus of crickets and frogs.

124

I used my cell phone as a flash light, shining it around a neatly manicured rock garden along the back of the house. It took a few minutes, but Dakota found the one perfectly shaped rock with a painted, porous texture on it.

She held up the key and it glinted in the dark, casting an eerie streak of light across the back lawn.

Winter and I took Dakota's lead, following her up to the back door while she unlocked it, then slipping inside. The room the door opened up into was a kitchen; I could see it barely only because of the moonlight. I waited for Dakota to locate the light switch, breathing out a sigh of relief when the kitchen light popped on.

I looked around the kitchen. There were a few dirty dishes in the sink. A week old newspaper on the table. *Where the hell was Sydney?*

We walked through each room on the bottom floor, seeing nothing out of the ordinary—besides the fact that everything looked unused, like no one had been here in weeks.

"Detective Simms said he saw signs of struggle. But I don't see anything down here, do you all?" I asked, peeking in a tiny one and a half bath off the living room.

"Nope," Winter said, staring at the twisted staircase leading upstairs.

We made our way upstairs to Sydney's bedroom. Seeing it again, only after being here a week ago, felt strange. We'd sat on her bed and talked. She was this living, breathing person and now she had simply vanished. And wherever she was, she was more than likely missing a tongue...

Bottles of perfume, makeup, and clothes were strewn across her bedroom...although her bed was perfectly made.

"Do you think she was sitting at the dresser when someone took her?" Dakota asked, her hands shaking as she reached down to touch Sydney's brushes and combs. "This must be where the struggle happened..."

"It almost looks that way...like someone yanked her out of her seat and knocked everything over in the process," Winter added.

"Or maybe Sydney knocked it all over while she was fighting like hell against the piece of shit who took her," I said angrily.

I opened her closet and dug through her drawers. Winter looked under the bed.

"She was such a neat freak," Winter said, sifting through a stack of magazines she'd pulled out from under the bed. *If I knew Sydney, they were organized according to date...*

"She *is* a neat freak. Not *was*." Dakota stared up from the floor at Winter, giving her the evil eye again.

"Sorry," Winter muttered.

Standing in front of Sydney's tall bureau drawer, I saw a cluster of silver and gold-framed photographs. There was a cheerleading picture of the whole team from last year, and a photograph of her with her parents. Behind those was a picture of a cute, little, old lady—the same one from Facebook I had messaged the other day—this must be Grandma Rose.

I lifted the photograph, staring at the woman in

question. I wondered why she hadn't messaged me back yet. It seemed strange. Most people check their Facebook accounts daily, but since she was old…maybe she didn't log on regularly.

We searched the upstairs bathrooms and Sydney's mom and dad's bedroom. I was hoping to find an address book or a list of extra out of town contact numbers, but again I came up empty.

"Nothing. This place is so beautiful but it's got no heart. Nothing in the drawers or cabinets, except for the bare necessities. I see why Sydney is the way she is. Her parents don't strike me as the nostalgic type. Or the type who spend much time *living* inside this house," Winter said.

By the time we made it back to my house, it was nearly four in the morning. We had to get up and go to school—unless it got called off again.

Dakota snuck back home, while Winter and I creeped up the creaky staircase, trying our best not to wake up my mom or grandma.

We collapsed on my bed, falling asleep instantly and not even bothering with setting the alarm.

***

I didn't open my eyes until nearly eleven in the morning. Thinking I was late, I crept downstairs, my eyes still adjusting for the day. I felt like I had a hangover, from lack of sleep and the stress of everything. *Had we really gone to Sydney's house last night?* In retrospect, it seemed so foolish.

My mom wasn't home, but Grandma Mimi was humming and knitting in the living room. I'd never seen her sew or knit before. It seemed almost too grandmotherly of an activity for her...

"I'm incredibly late for school," I croaked, my voice strained and raspy from lack of sleep.

"It got called off again. The police are treating it like a crime scene again, trying to get some prints off of that box with the tongue in it," Grandma said.

"Was it on the news?" I asked, staring at the turned off television in the corner.

"Yep. I needed a break from it all." Grandma Mimi kept knitting, resuming her humming as I went upstairs to wake up Winter.

"I better head home. I left a note last night, but I'm sure my mom will be pissed that I left without waking her up. Thanks for letting me stay. And, Amanda? I'm sorry we didn't find anything to help Sydney. I didn't know her well—*don't* know her well—but she seemed very smart and kind." Winter gave me a sad, sorry look.

I nodded, pursing my lips.

After Winter left, I seriously considered climbing back in bed. *To hell with this day*, I thought, sitting on the edge of the bed and twisting the covers in my fists.

I felt like I needed to be doing something, *anything*, to help my missing friend.

Pulling out my cell phone, I was surprised to see a new message in my inbox from someone on Facebook. Quickly opening it, I was happy to see Sydney's Grandma Rose has responded.

Rose: *I'm so sorry about your friend, hun. I have lots of friends on FB, but I don't know*

128

most of them personally. Sydney seems like a sweet young girl, but she is not my granddaughter. Maybe in another life she would be, you never know. Good luck finding your friend, sweetheart. If there's any way I can help, please let me know and I will.

I stared at her response in shock. Clicking on her profile pic, I felt certain she was the same woman in the framed photograph on Sydney's dresser.

The hair on my arms stood up and I shivered, gripping the blankets around me for warmth.

Why would Sydney lie about having a grandmother named Rose? Furthermore, why in the world would she put a stranger's picture in a frame and call the stranger her grandmother?

Chapter Thirty-Three

According to Grandma Mimi, my mom was out looking for a job. Job hunting for so long seemed unlikely, and by the time six o'clock rolled around, I was certain she was never coming back again.

It wouldn't be the first time she said she was going somewhere and then didn't show up again for several months.

I baked cookies to distract myself, kneading the dough with a vengeance and angrily cutting out heart shaped pieces from the flattened dough.

But then the gooey little white pieces reminded me of Genevieve's nose…

The news was on in the living room. When I heard a local correspondent say the words, "breaking news," I set down the knife and joined Grandma Mimi on the couch.

"After much investigation, a source in the Harrow Hill police department confirmed what we've all suspected. Genevieve McDermott was murdered. A blow to the back of the head is what killed her. All other injuries were sustained postmortem."

I let out a sigh of relief. *At least they didn't cut off her nose while she was still alive.*

The fact that *that* was comforting, made me realize how bad things had really gotten.

"There's a killer on the loose in Harrow Hill. Police suspect the same person who killed Miss McDermott also kidnapped another young student, Sydney Hargreaves. A terrifying note and tongue were planted in another girl's locker, along with a note leading us to believe that the tongue belonged to our missing girl. But sources now say the tongue did not belong to a human. The tongue appears to be from the porcine family…or in other words, it came from a pig."

The reporter kept talking, but I couldn't hear anything else. I was hit by a flood of emotions.

Relief that the tongue didn't belong to Sydney…but something was off about this.

What did Sydney say the other day when we were running late to school?

Suddenly recalling the details, I repeated her words aloud: "I'm dissecting a pig today."

Chapter Thirty-Four

I was surprised to find my mom sleeping on the living room couch the next morning, bundled up in a fetal position and under a blanket. She appeared to be sweating profusely.

I rolled my eyes at her, heading for the front door. I had plans today—important ones.

"Where are you going?" With one eye open, my mom sat up from the couch, looking at me, confused.

"I have to run some errands," I said vaguely, slipping my feet back in the dew-dampened Keds from last night.

"Going where, exactly?" she asked, rubbing sleep from her eyes and pushing the blankets aside.

"What business is it of yours? You were gone all day and night yesterday. How about I ask you some questions? For starters, where were you all day yesterday, and why the hell did you even bother coming back?" I asked, sounding harsher than I'd anticipated.

What came next surprised me.

"I was having an evaluation done at the hospital. I've been accepted into a drug treatment program but there won't be a bed available for me for another week. I'm trying to dry out, honey. I want to get better for you."

Momentarily forgetting my plans, I took a cautious step toward her. I wanted to believe her...I did.

But she'd disappointed me so many times before...

"Why did you ever start using in the first place?" I asked, afraid to even hear her answer. *What if it was because raising me was too stressful? Was I to blame for her desperate need to numb the pain?*

"Baby, life is complicated. *People* are complicated. I was so young when I had you. Young and childish. Your dad was in a band and I thought he was so damn cool. I'd have done anything to impress him. That's when the addiction started. It became less of a fun activity and more of a necessity to function," she explained.

"So it wasn't because of me...? It wasn't my fault you all struggled with money and used drugs...? My fault Dad did what he did?"

She looked stunned by my questions. "Oh, honey. I'm so sorry you ever thought that. Absolutely not! You are the only reason I ever stopped using. The only motivation to be good. I want to be someone you admire, someone you can look up to someday. I want you to be proud of me."

"I'll be proud of you if you get clean, Mom."

133

"I will. I won't promise you because I always promise and break it...but I am going to get clean." She said it with such conviction, for me but also for herself.

We hugged, and for the first time in a long time, I saw her for who she was—my mother...imperfect in every way possible, but my mother nevertheless. I'd never loved her more.

"I need to get going," I said, standing up and wiping wetness from eyes.

"Will you tell me where you're really going?" my mom asked, eyeing me suspiciously.

"I will, but you're not going to like it."

"Try me," she said.

"I'm going to see Ashleigh Westerfield, the girl who tried to kill Sydney last year. I called juvenile detention. She's allowed visitors today. There are some questions I need to ask her."

My mom raised her eyebrows, surprised. "Let me get my purse and I'll take you," she said, surprising me.

Chapter Thirty-Five

I expected Crimson County's juvenile detention center to be scary and hulking. Instead, it was a small round building, filled with "cells" that more closely resembled small dorm rooms than locked cages.

My mother and I waited patiently at the main desk in the center, watching "inmates" come and go from their rooms freely. There was a quaint sitting room, equipped with a fancy flat screen television and a work station with a decent-looking computer and monitor.

It was hard to believe this place could be used as a form of punishment...but at the same time, I guess being kept away from school, family, friends, and everyday normal society was punishment enough in itself.

"This way please," said a cute male orderly, who was sporting a tiny mustache that looked freshly grown on his youthful face.

The three of us stood outside a "cell" with the number eight painted on the side next to its door frame. With the scan of a keycard and a small buzzing sound, we were led inside a girl's bedroom. Ashleigh Westerfield sat on the bed, drawing.

She barely glanced up at us, much to my surprise. Her cream colored walls were covered in sketches. Some of them were drawings of cheerleaders, a big letter D—for Dragons, I presumed—displayed proudly on the chest of their uniforms.

"You have about fifteen minutes," the orderly said, giving me an apologetic look. He walked out, leaving Mom and me alone with Ashleigh, although he did leave the door to the room propped open. Across the hallway, I could see several staff members patrolling. That gave me a greater sense of safety.

"Ashleigh, its's Amanda. Do you remember me from school?"

She stopped drawing and looked up, seemingly catching my words. She nodded, a strange, gleeful expression on her face. "How's the team doing?" she asked, surprising me.

My mom gave me a strange look, raising her eyebrows questioningly.

"Can you leave us alone for a few minutes?" I asked her. Mom looked like she wanted to say no, but finally, she backed out of the room, never taking her eyes off of Ashleigh. "I'll be right in the hallway if you need me," she warned.

Ashleigh watched me as I took a seat, pulling the chair close to where she sat on the bed. Her expression was friendly, genuine. She looked wide-eyed and eager…almost *innocent*.

"Things are not well, actually. Now there's a new person harassing us. I was hoping you could help me figure it out," I said.

"How can I help from in here?" Ashleigh asked, looking around her small eight by six room.

"*Why* did you do it, Ashleigh? Why did you stalk us and try to kill Sydney? Can you at least tell me that?" I pleaded.

I expected her demeanor to change. But her smile never faded, almost like it was painted on.

She reminded me of a ventriloquist dummy, one of those bizarre-looking ones that always seemed to be in a perpetual state of creepy bliss.

Ashley's expression turned serious. "You want to know *why*? Well, that's easy. I put Sydney in the locker because she told me to. She wanted me to stop her because she couldn't stop herself."

I felt the air leave my lungs. "What do you mean?" I demanded, still not registering her words.

"Sydney told me to stuff her in the locker. She told me to do all of those things. She said I had to do it, for the team."

Chapter Thirty-Six

"Mom. Let's go home," I breathed, nearly tripping over myself on the way out of the door. The walls of the detention center were wavy, distorted. I felt disconnected, like the world wasn't real anymore.

When I was little, I used to literally believe that the world revolved around me. My life was like *The Truman Show*, everyone watching and playing their role in this movie I called *My Life*. I used to pretend my decisions and actions could influence the entire planet.

I think I wanted to believe it because I felt so insignificant and small. By playing that silly game, I could make even the most unbearable days have meaning.

Today felt like one of those days. I stumbled through the hallway, people staring at me strangely.

The world is a stage, and everyone is laughing...

When we finally burst through the exit doors, I

desperately sucked in air, trying to fill my lungs and calm my rapid heartbeat.

What did this new knowledge mean? And did it mean what I thought it meant?

My mom reached across the seat of Grandma's classic car, pulling my seatbelt across my lap for me. She hooked it in, then just stared. "Talk to me, Amanda. Talk to me now. Are you all right? What did that girl say to you?"

"Nothing. It was just so upsetting for me to see her, is all…" I breathed, trying to recover.

I had to go to Detective Simms. I had to tell Mom and Grandma. I had to tell Dakota too. But I wasn't ready to do it just yet.

Somewhere in the distance, Mom was offering to take me to Kentucky Fried Chicken. "Want a bucket of chicken?" she asked, her voice sounding far away.

"Can we just go straight home? I'm really tired."

"Okay." My mom was quiet and pensive, wanting to ask more but apparently deciding not to. I was grateful she didn't. We listened to the radio, local news about sports and upcoming events.

"This just in—we have breaking news." The young female reporter's voice woke me from my trance—the reporter sounded excited as she fumbled for a few minutes, obviously live and unscripted.

"The young girl reported missing—Sydney Michelle Hargreaves—has been found. Stay tuned for details after these messages from our sponsors."

"What?" I screamed at the speaker. I pounded it with my fists, willing her to come back on. By now, my mom had pulled over on the side of the road. She reached for my arms, trying to calm me down.

"Is she dead? Did they find her body? Is she alive? Come on!" I screamed at an advertisement for itch relief cream.

"Just wait and listen," my mom whispered, turning up the volume on the radio.

"Okay, Kelly Fenteel back again. This just in—Sydney Hargreaves has miraculously been found. And, get this folks! She's alive! She walked back into town bruised and bloody, but essentially nothing broken and most importantly, *alive*! Apparently, her captor had a change of heart and decided to let her go. She is currently with police, and more details are soon to follow...now here's an old favorite, "Paint it Black" by the Rolling Stones..."

"That's wonderful news, honey. Do you want me to drive you down to the police station to see her now?" my mom asked, an expression of wonderment on her face.

I shook my head, still staring at the speaker, which sung of red doors and the need to paint the whole world black. I wanted to listen to this song...

I needed to know more about my missing friend and how she'd been found...but the music kept playing, its addicting, haunting lyrics sucking me in...

"You want to go home then? Honey, I'm sorry you're upset. This has all been so hard on you..."

"Mom?"

"Yes, honey?" She was staring at me now, her face twisted up with worry and concern.

I was feeling pretty worried myself.

I pulled myself away from the music and looked at my mother, my face grave.

"Mom. She did it. Sydney is the one who killed Genevieve, the one who tried to kill Brittani, and threatened me. It's been Sydney all along."

Chapter Thirty-Seven

Sitting across from my mom and Grandma Mimi, I told them exactly why I thought Sydney did it.

"First of all, Ashleigh *told me* that Sydney made her do it."

"Made her stuff Sydney into a locker and try to kill her? Made her kill a cat and stuff it in Brittani's bag last year? That just doesn't make sense, honey. Not to mention the fact that the girl is a little unstable…" my mom protested.

"Listen to the girl, Bethany!" Grandma Mimi snapped at my mother.

Giving me a sheepish grimace, my mother encouraged me to go on.

"There's this picture of Sydney's Grandma Rose on her dresser. This same lady is on her Facebook page, although the lady claims she doesn't know Sydney in real life."

Pulling up Rose's profile, I showed it to my

mom and grandma.

"She has a fake Grandma Rose."

When they didn't say anything, I went on, "And right before she went missing, Sydney was doing a pig dissection in advanced bio. The tongue in Winter's locker belonged to a pig."

My mom and grandma exchanged worried looks.

"So, you're saying Sydney killed Genevieve and did all of those other things, even faking her *own* kidnapping, all the while she was responsible for what happened last year too…?" my mother asked, disbelievingly.

I couldn't blame her. I didn't want to believe it either. But I've always been a stickler for the facts. There were too many coincidences not to suspect Sydney at this point.

"What should we do now?" Grandma Mimi asked, her voice hushed and frightened.

"First, we should—"

There was a loud banging sound at the front door.

"Oh my God, I bet it's Sydney!" I hissed.

Chapter Thirty-Eight

When I peeked through the peephole, I was surprised to see Jordan outside. I opened the door, staring at him crossly. He was holding the baby doll by one arm, swinging it side to side.

"Can you take this baby for a bit? I need to go to practice and study for a bit." He looked tired, his face gaunt with circles under his eyes.

I fought the urge to slam the door in his face.

"Is *she* going with you to practice?" I asked, pointing out to his car, where I could see Lauren perched in the passenger's seat, painting her perfect little toenails.

"*Well*, we're going to get something to eat first, but then I have to practice. Our first game is next week. I told you I'm going to break up with her soon…"

I reached out and grabbed the baby from his hands. "For the record, you're a terrible boyfriend *and* a terrible father." I slammed the door in his face.

My mom and grandma were struggling not to laugh, but I wasn't in the mood for jokes.

"We need to call Detective Simms and tell him about Sydney before she hurts anyone else," I said solemnly.

Chapter
Thirty-Nine

Bouncing Baby Annie on my lap, I regurgitated my theories to Detective Simms. He listened, his face unmoving, not giving away his thoughts.

Does he believe me?

It was hard to know for certain. Mom and Grandma Mimi were standing in the kitchen, leaning against the counter.

"And Ashleigh told me, 'Sydney made me do it'. So, all this time she's been sitting in there, all the while she's innocent! And Sydney's been playing some screwed up mind game with all of us!"

"I'll look into it," Detective Simms said, pushing back his chair with a screech.

"Wait! That's it?" *He doesn't believe me*, I realized, my face heating up with anger and embarrassment.

"That's it for now. I have to go talk to Sydney," he said flatly.

"Is she back home?" I asked, a nervous flutter

filling my stomach.

"She's at the station, still giving her statement."

"Did she tell you who supposedly kidnapped her?" I asked, scared for him to leave. I didn't want to be wrong about this, because if I was wrong, then I really *was* crazy...

"She did. It was someone wearing a mask. Similar to the masked person Brittani described. They didn't hurt her, only held her hostage for a few days..."

"Who was it? Do you know?" I asked, standing up beside him. I handed off Baby Annie to my mom.

"We can't release any more information at this time."

Chapter Forty

I stood under the shower head, letting the hot water run over my face and body, keeping the temperature hot enough to burn my skin.

Filled with doubts, I closed my eyes, trying to think about the last conversation I had with Sydney.

"Amanda, open up!" Dakota shouted through the bathroom door, startling me and interrupting my thoughts.

I turned the water off and stepped out, drying off quickly with a still-damp towel from this morning.

When I opened the door, Dakota was standing in the hallway smiling.

"Did you hear the news?"

Before I could answer, she flung her arms around me, pulling me in for a hug so fast I nearly dropped my towel on the floor.

"Get dressed. We're going to see her. She's at the station. And guess what? Her tongue is still intact. I was right...this asshole who's been harassing us is all talk. A stupid prankster," she said.

148

"Would you call Genevieve getting murdered "all talk"?" I asked, stunned.

Remembering Genevieve, Dakota frowned. "Well, not in her case...no. You're right. But aren't you happy Sydney's all right? I didn't want to say it out loud before, Amanda...but I was really starting to think she was dead."

Unsure of how to break the news to Dakota, I pulled on a pair of orange leggings and a thin grey tee. The only shoes I could find were my worn out flip flops, but I slid them on anyway and pulled my wet hair up in a ponytail.

"Ready?" Dakota asked, pacing excitedly around my room.

"I think so," I said, grabbing my purse and following her downstairs.

"I'm going with Dakota to talk to Sydney at the station," I told Mom and Grandma. They were still sitting at the table, talking quietly over cups of coffee. My mom looked up, alarmed.

"Let me get my shoes on," she said, starting to get up.

"No, I need to do this on my own. I need to talk to Sydney. I'll be safe. It's a police station." I looked at Grandma Mimi. She nodded her consent, urging my mom back down in her seat.

"Why are you acting so weird?" Dakota asked as we climbed in the Cavalier.

"I have something to tell you," I said, taking a deep breath before I told my theories for a third time today.

Chapter Forty-One

"Get out of my car."

Shocked, I sat frozen in the passenger's seat of Dakota's car, unsure what I should do.

Dakota made my decision for me. "Get. The. Hell. Out," she angrily demanded.

This wasn't the reaction I'd expected. Disbelief, yes. But downright hostility? No. I didn't expect this at all…

Hastily, I unfastened my seatbelt and climbed out, holding Baby Annie and my purse. I watched Dakota pull away without a second thought, burning rubber on her car's new tires in the process.

Defeated, I turned back toward my house, walking slowly and ignoring the baby's cries.

The sun was nowhere to be seen, a storm brewing in Harrow Hill. Wind whipped through the trees, sending a chill across my skin and through my bones.

I regretted not bringing a jacket or wearing

normal shoes. It was September and that's usually a warm month around here, but tonight the air felt cold and damp.

I crossed Brixton Avenue, taking a shortcut through a few neighbors' yards. I was two blocks from my house when I heard a car coming up behind me.

Part of me hoped it was Dakota...maybe she'd changed her mind...

But the girl who pulled up beside me had long, curly, red hair and bright green eyes. I scowled at Mariella Martin.

"Get in. I'll drive you home," she said.

I hesitated, then kept walking.

"Do you really hate me that much? You won't even accept a ride from me? I heard about Sydney. Are you okay?" Mariella inched along beside me.

She heard what *about Sydney?*

Making a quick decision, I turned around and walked around the car to the passenger side door.

It was a cute two-door car with fancy necklaces dangling around the rearview mirror and a stack of boy band CDs crudely stacked in the center console.

Mariella smiled at my decision, pulling off and heading toward my house.

"What did you hear about Sydney?" I asked.

Mariella glanced at me, her lips parting in surprise.

"She was just arrested."

I gasped. I'd expected Detective Simms to question her, but I didn't really think he believed me.

"Dakota is on her way to the station to see

her…" I realized, talking out loud.

"If she sees her, it will be in handcuffs. She was charged with Genevieve's murder and attempted murder too. Not only did the police find no evidence that she'd been kidnapped, but they traced her back to a hotel in Crimson County, *and* they found a crowbar in her bedroom."

"*Where* in her room?" I asked, instantly feeling uneasy.

"Under her bed, of all places!" Mariella pulled up in front of Grandma Mimi's house, shaking her head back and forth as she parked.

"For someone so stupid, she sure she was dumb…who leaves a bloody murder weapon right under their bed? And I know some people didn't like Genevieve, but who knew Sydney was so unhinged…"

Mariella rambled on, but my mind was spinning. *Me, Winter, and Dakota were in Sydney's house a couple nights ago and there was* definitely *no crow bar under her bed…right?*

"And her parents just got in from Prague. Those assholes didn't even know their own daughter was missing! I actually feel a little bad for her. No wonder she was sort of screwed up, negligent parents and all that…" Mariella rambled.

"Thanks for the ride," I said, darting out the passenger side and running into the house.

I closed the front door of the house behind me, panting.

I was wrong. The police had the wrong girl. Someone must have set Sydney up.

Chapter Forty-Two

Jordan was waiting for me, leaning up against the locker in a handsome green polo and Lucky jeans.

I'm not in the mood for this crap...

Ignoring him, I turned the dial to my locker, lifting up on the lock to open it. I started pulling out books for my morning classes, trying not to look at Jordan.

He spoke, his breath smelling like peppermint and something chocolate...

"I'm sorry about the other night, Amanda. I didn't mean to hurt your feelings. And I should have helped out more with the Child Development project, I'll admit...but I want you to know that I *am* still planning to break up with Lauren, so don't worry...you are the next girl I want to be with," Jordan said.

I scoffed at him.

Seriously, where did this guy get the nerve?

153

And speaking of girlfriends, I could see Lauren moving through the hallway, pure perfection in a baby doll tee with the words **"Kiss me"** sewn on the front. She wasn't the most humble person in the world, and she was so...*annoyingly perfect*. But she still didn't deserve to be treated like this. She could do better than this asshole. *And so could I, for that matter.*

"Listen Jordan, even if you break up with Lauren, I will *never* be interested in dating you," I said, slamming my locker shut.

Jordan looked shocked, his lips tensing and eyes narrowing.

His initially confused expression turned to one of anger.

"I knew what everyone said about you was true! You are crazy, like your dead dad!" he said, stomping off to chase after Lauren.

It wasn't the first time someone had used my past against me to hurt my feelings. But for some reason, this time it bounced right off. *I don't know what I ever saw in that guy...*

Good riddance, Jordan.

Chapter Forty-Three

The Sociopath

Dear Ashleigh,

Once again, you pulled off a great performance. Amanda believed your story hook, line, and sinker. I owe you big time for this one...

We did it. We got away with murder and framed that bitch Sydney in the process. The only name they'll find on the receipt to the hotel will be Sydney's...

You should be released any day now, just in time for cheerleading tryouts...then you can claim your rightful position on the squad. Finally. I told you this day *would come.*

Go Dragons!

xoxoxoxoxoxoxo

Chapter
Forty-Four

Amanda

3 weeks later...

As much as I hated to admit it, life at Harrow High had been quiet since Sydney's arrest. Life was returning to normal, events from a few weeks ago nearly forgotten. School was business as usual—chemistry tests, pop quizzes, and plans underway for the annual homecoming dance...

But there was one thing that wasn't normal...Dakota still wouldn't talk to me. Not even once since that night in her car.

I missed my friend...and not just Dakota. I missed Sydney too. I stared at her empty seat in Brit Lit and thought about her at lunchtime. *What kind of food do they serve in juvenile detention?*

Sydney was so picky and health conscious. I couldn't imagine her liking anything they served

157

besides lettuce or other vegetables…

Did she see Ashleigh often? Were they bunkmates? Arch enemies?

Best friends?

After three weeks of getting life back on track, Coach Davis finally made the announcement— cheerleading tryouts would be held today after school. We had one shot to impress her, and one shot only. Tomorrow morning she would announce the six girls who made it, and two girls who would serve as alternates.

We had already missed two pre-games, and Coach Davis—although wanting to give us adequate time to mourn Genevieve and recover from the shock that Sydney killed her—needed to make her choices and get us prepped to cheer for the upcoming games. Not to mention the competition in Dallas this June…

The day moved slowly, anticipation building for what Coach Davis had in store for us…

I made my way down to the gym, walking alone as usual. The last time I'd done this on the first day of tryouts, I'd found a dead body in the locker room.

Shuddering, I waited for other girls to enter the gym before I walked into the locker room to get changed. Lauren, Blakely, and Mariella were getting dressed, talking amongst themselves.

They got quiet when they saw me come in.

Frowning, I found a semi-private corner of the locker room and quickly changed into my tights and sports bra.

I wonder what that was all about…

I stuffed my feet in my tennis shoes and pushed my way through another gang of freshman girls. Standing on the other side of the door was Dakota. My eyes widening, I let out a cry of dismay.

Standing behind Dakota was Ashleigh Westerfield.

Chapter
Forty-Five

"Watch out! Ashleigh's behind you!" I shouted to Dakota. Images of Ashleigh stabbing her in the back flashed before my eyes…

"I know. You're the one who pointed the finger at Sydney, remember? Ashleigh's innocent, according to the police. And she's been back for days now. What rock have you been living under?" Dakota stared at me with a blank, tired expression.

Ashleigh obviously heard us talking, but she politely excused herself, slipping past us to go in the locker room. There were more hushed whispers about Ashleigh coming from the other girls in the gym.

"I guess when you don't have any friends, it's easy to miss out on current events." Dakota tried to move past me too, but I moved over, blocking her path.

"Please, Dakota. I don't want to fight with you. I'm really sorry. But all signs pointed to…"

160

I couldn't even get Sydney's name out.

"You're a traitor, simple as that. Now move out of my way! I have to get ready for tryouts. And by the way, I *don't* wish you luck!"

It was stupid and childish, but it hurt all the same. *How could she be so mad at me?*

I remembered the first day of school, Sydney taking her side over mine...Dakota was the same way. They were close, and would always choose each other's friendship over mine.

It hurt. But I had to move on and focus on tryouts.

I took a seat on the bench, waiting for the other girls to come sit beside me. Coach Davis came in, giving me a familiar wave, just as Lauren came plunging across the gym, showing off her double back hand spring and ending with a full.

So much for being humble...

I got off the bench and started stretching. Winter joined me, smiling and perky as ever. Brittani Barlow came over too, strangely wearing a thin knit turtleneck. To cover up her neck, I supposed...

Brittani looked around the gym wildly, still paranoid despite Sydney's arrest.

Dakota came out of the locker room and took her spot on the floor—which was as far away from me as possible.

Maybe I don't have many friends and maybe Dakota hates me...but I'm going to make the squad, one way or another, I decided. *At this point, it's all I had left to look forward to.*

Chapter Forty-Six

Coach Davis made a short announcement about Ashleigh trying out for the team. She was stretching alongside Blakely and Mariella, and seeing her made me feel sick to my stomach. Maybe she wasn't the mastermind, but she was definitely involved in hurting my friends, I could feel it in my gut. And anyone who stuffs someone in a locker to suffocate just because someone told them to do it cannot be trusted.

"Ashleigh has been cleared of all charges. She deserves to be treated with respect, and like everyone else here, she will get her fair shot at making the team," Coach Davis said sternly, looking at each of us in turn.

We all nodded in agreement, even me.

Everyone was quiet, trying not to look at Ashleigh. But I was looking…she was smiling, her expression…almost triumphant.

Ugh.

"Everybody on the line, at least a leg-length apart!" Coach Davis commanded.

We lined up as directed, making sure to leave enough room to perform a tumble or jump.

"The next thirty minutes will be intense. This is an accelerated version of tryouts."

Coach Davis paced up and down in front of our line, holding the whistle around her neck close to her lips.

"I will tell you what to do and how many sets to do. When I blow my whistle, you will begin and not stop until I blow it again."

"Toe-touch. Ten sets. Go." She blew the whistle.

Lifting my arms in a V, I did my first toe-touch and transitioned into the second.

One expression came to mind—*Welcome to Hell.*

Chapter
Forty-Seven

After ten sets of each jump, Coach Davis had us perform standing back handsprings and then back tucks. Just when I thought we were finished, she ordered us to do push-ups and run in place as fast and as hard as we could.

Some of the girls performed admirably, their jumps and tumbles flawless. Others struggled and a couple stopped before the next whistle sounded. I tried to keep an eye on my competition, but I was too focused on nailing my own moves to see much.

"Take a ten minute break and hydrate. When we get back, I'll teach you a cheer and a lift. That will be your final test for the day," Coach Davis said.

I was sweating and already sore as hell as I grabbed a drink of water from the fountain. I watched Dakota talking to Lauren and Blakely. She seemed to be doing just fine without me.

"Hey, stranger." Winter stood behind me, waiting for her turn at the water fountain. "You haven't been taking my calls," she whined.

I moved aside, letting her get a drink. "I'm sorry, I've just been upset about Sydney. And Dakota's not talking to me, so I don't know why you would."

"Because we're friends, silly. And because you can talk to me anytime. I'm here for you, Amanda. I don't know if Sydney really did it or not, but I know you wouldn't make things up just to hurt her. There was enough evidence against her for the police to believe it, so maybe Dakota should be apologizing to *you*," Winter said.

I didn't see that happening anytime soon...

Jogging back over to the group, I joined a staggered line of girls to learn the individual cheer. The hardest part over, I felt sure I could nail this part.

***

My mom left for rehab this morning, so I didn't have a ride home from school. I should have asked Grandma Mimi to pick me up, but I knew it would cause her a great deal of anxiety, leaving the house like that. So, I started walking home, happy that the sun was warm and gleaming bright.

Sure, I lived nearly six miles from school, but the exercise wouldn't hurt me. If I was going to cheer on Coach Davis's squad this year, I needed to get in better shape anyway. She was turning out to be one tough coach this year!

Cars swished by, leaving me behind on the sidewalk of Harrow's main street. I kept my eyes to the ground, thinking about cheerleading and wondering when my mom would be home.

Even though I didn't fully trust her, I was proud of her decision to go to rehab. At least she was trying to get better.

A flash of red caught my attention and I watched the taillights of Dakota's Cavalier grow smaller and smaller in the distance.

"Hey, hop in!"

It was Jordan's car, but Winter was the one shouting out of the passenger side window. I glanced over, slowing down. Jordan was driving and Lauren was in the back. She shot me a tight smile.

I hadn't talked to Jordan much either. "We" aced the parent project, although I was the one who did all the work.

I should have known from the beginning he was a player…apparently, he'd been hitting on a couple other girls in our Child Development class too, or so I'd heard…

What did I ever see in that guy?

"Nah. I feel like walking, but thanks anyway," I said, waving them off.

"You sure?" Winter asked, looking worried. More cars were coming up behind Jordan's car, honking their horns angrily at Jordan for blocking the road.

"No, go ahead. I need the air," I answered.

I watched as they too disappeared in the distance.

I missed my mom. A lot.

That's something I wouldn't have imagined just a couple months ago…

But her being back…I'd grown attached. *How*

long? I'd asked her. But she didn't have an answer.

"Everyone is different," she'd told me. *It might take six weeks or six years for her to get fully clean.* I prayed for it to be the former.

I had tried to go see her at the rehab center, but they turned me away at the door. "She's detoxing, and what that means is she's not in a state where she can see people yet. We don't allow visitors, even family, for the first ninety days. It's usually in the patient's best interest, and it's protocol here…"

It seemed like a harsh policy, and definitely one I didn't like. But if *not* seeing her for a while would help her, then so be it—I wouldn't visit.

After all, I had spent so much of my life without her. *What was a few more months, really?*

"Can you leave her a message for me?" I had quietly asked the nurse.

The nurse looked skeptical, but finally said she would.

"Just tell her that I love her. And if she screws up again and relapses, please tell her not to run away this time. Screwed up or not, I want her around. I don't want her to leave again. Oh, and tell her I'm proud of her…"

The nurse promised to relay the message.

"Get in," said another hoarse voice, pulling up next to me and breaking my train of thought. In my deep thoughts, I had barely noticed Grandma Mimi's car. It was only the second time I had ever seen her drive, and she looked strange sitting behind the wheel.

Sitting in a car period…

I happily climbed in, my legs aching from Coach

Davis's brutal tryouts.

Chapter
Forty-Eight

Seeing Grandma Mimi drive was like catching a glimpse of the Hubble telescope in the sky. I enjoyed watching her, the way her tiny porcelain hands grasped the wheel. She was so short that she sat on the edge of the seat, her nose tipped up as she struggled to see the road over the wheel. Her face was filled with tiny wrinkle lines and age spots, but I never doubted the fact that once upon a time, Grandma Mimi was a beautiful girl.

I'd seen pictures of her, with a fancy headdress and jeweled leotard, kicking out her legs in a glamorous pose. I'd seen silly shots of her and my dad when he was little and she was young. Her hair, now white and cut short, was once long and silky, white-blonde. Her eyes were one thing that still hadn't aged—they were so blue, like tiny rare crystals.

She saw me staring and smiled.

"Why do you hide away, always staying in the

169

house?" I asked her.

It was a random question, but one I'd wanted to ask for years now. I barely knew her when I was young, not until I was placed in her care. But now that I did know her, I wanted to know more about her and the life that led to her hiding in the house all day.

"I'm not hiding. I'm settling."

She said it so simply, as though that were enough to fulfill my curiosity.

When she saw that it wasn't enough, she went on: "I ran around, and was barely around to care for your father...you see, I wasn't suited for motherhood. I lived a glamorous life, filled with money and fame and important people. I thought it was what I wanted. I thought it was the most important thing. But the truth be told, none of it ever really mattered. Your father grew up and his father—my husband—died. And I missed out on everything. I thought I had so much time to settle down. But sometimes all you have to do is blink and it's over...life, that is..."

"But *I'm* here now, Grandma. Your life isn't over," I pointed out, suddenly softening to the pained expression on her face. "What my father did, in that bank...it wasn't your fault, Grandma Mimi," I added.

Taking her eyes off the road, she looked at me, shocked. "Of course it was."

I didn't know what to say, so I didn't say anything. We rode home in silence until we were pulling in the driveway.

"There's a letter for you on the kitchen table,"

170

she said briskly.

"From who?" I asked. But she didn't answer. She got out of the car and went inside, locking herself in her room again.

I stood in the kitchen, staring at the letter on the table. It was addressed to me and it was stamped with Crimson County Juvenile Hall's address.

Taking a deep breath, I ripped it open and sat down to read Sydney's letter.

Dear Amanda,

I know we haven't been friends for long, but it feels like I've known you forever. I've always admired you, growing up without parents to care for you. I never realized it before, but...you and I are a lot alike. More alike than you probably know.

I know it's different...my parents have money and I've always grown up having nice things. But the truth is, they've never been around. They buy me things and leave me money, but they live their own life, a life dedicated to their careers.

I'm lonely. In here, at home, wherever I go...

In a room full of people, I still feel lonely.

There's only one person I've ever had, and that was Dakota. At first, when you came in the picture, I'll admit it—I was jealous.

But then I realized how cool you were and suddenly, I had two best friends. I felt less lonely than I ever have.

Amanda, I'm not mad at you for the things you said to Detective Simms. My Grandma Rose—the one you talked to on Facebook? She has something called Alzheimer's disease. She doesn't remember who I am—or anyone—most days. I did dissect a pig in Advanced Biology, but so did five other classes and anyone could have gained access to the lab. Mrs. Faulklin rarely even locks the room to her classroom.

I never hurt Genevieve, although I'll admit I've never liked her. You know how smart I am: would I leave a bloody crowbar under my bed? If I was going to "fake" my own kidnapping, would I take out a motel reservation in my name? No way! I'm not that stupid!

Someone set me up.

The only part I can't figure out is why Ashleigh would tell you that. Why in the world she would say I told her to try to kill me last year...or to pretend to kill me. It makes no sense.

Unless she's got a reason to set me

up...

I'll be honest, Amanda. I don't think Ashleigh is the one behind all of the pranks last year and this year. Well, they're way more than pranks at this point, don't you think?

I don't think she did a lot of those things; she couldn't have done some of the recent stunts because she was locked up.

The person who kidnapped me...they locked me up in a basement and kept me blindfolded. I couldn't see my captor and I never heard that person speak. But one thing, I did notice—SHE was wearing heavy perfume. Her touch, her smell...left no doubt: "the sociopath" is a female.

Amanda, please be careful. I think there's someone at Harrow High pulling the strings and we're all the puppets.

Someone who hates school, and really hates the cheerleaders in particular.

Someone who took advantage of a weak person like Ashleigh Westerfield just to toy with us.

I'm afraid something really bad is going to happen, something worse than what already has...

I have this awful feeling that I just

can't shake.

Please know that I'm not mad at you. Just please...keep Dakota safe for me and don't forget to watch your back. You guys are all that I have, my one true family in this world.

Love,

Sydney

Chapter Forty-Nine

I tossed and turned all night, getting up out of bed to reread Sydney's letter nearly a dozen times. *Could it really be true? Her grandma had that disease that impacts your memory?*

If what she said was true, the police would figure it out and release her any day now. And that was a good thing...

But the bad thing—if Sydney wasn't the killer, then that meant the real killer was still out there, lying low and waiting to strike again.

Chapter Fifty

I was up before six in the morning, leaving one message after another for Detective Simms. "Please call me. It's an emergency. You guys have the wrong girl..." I said to his voicemail box for the fifth time before getting dressed for school.

I rode the bus in silence, staring out at the streets of Harrow Hill, wondering how I could have been so stupid to assume my best friend could do such horrible things...

By the time I got to first period, I was so deep in thought that when Principal Barlow came on over the intercom, I had no clue she was about to announce the results of cheerleading tryouts.

I'd forgotten all about cheerleading announcements...

I sat up straight in my seat, trying to force myself to get excited, or in the very least *nervous*.

But I was just too worried about my friend to focus on something as frivolous as cheerleading.

"Attention, students. I would like to announce the following six girls who have made the team, as

176

well as the two alternates I've chosen," Coach Davis said, taking over the mic from Principal Barlow.

"Congratulations to…Winter Addams, Brittani Barlow, Blakely Clovers, Lauren Delancey, Dakota Densford, and finally…"

Finally, I was listening. I braced my hands on the sides of my desk.

"Amanda Loxx," Coach finished. I let out a sigh of relief, realizing making the team meant more to me than I thought.

The intercom crackled and Coach Davis continued with her announcement:

"The following two girls have been chosen as alternates. Congratulations to Ashleigh Westerfield and Gabriella Michaels. The six girls I've chosen should stay after school tomorrow to get fitted for your uniforms. In addition to uniforms, we will be practicing. We must get straight to work, girls…we need to catch up for the time we have lost this season."

My classmates congratulated me and Winter. Winter was beaming ear to ear, thrilled to be chosen for the team. She nudged me across the aisle. "Smile! You just made the cheerleading team, silly!"

I did smile, but it definitely felt forced. I couldn't help thinking about Sydney, and how I'd cost her a spot on the team…

I spent the rest of the school day trying to enjoy the moment, but falling short every time…I had to get a hold of Detective Simms and make sure Sydney was released. That was my only concern for the time being.

Chapter Fifty-One

The Sociopath

I laid out my clothes for school, careful to smooth out the wrinkles in my black shirt and pants. I lined up my black combat boots side by side, wiping off smudges on the heels.

Then I laid out my black ski mask and gloves, along with the note I had written.

But most importantly, I had to get my backpack ready and what I was packing inside...

I stared at the note, my choppy writing, enjoying the words I had written:

> *Bang Bang choo choo train*
> *Watch the Dragons do their thang!*
> *The crowbar, the knife*
> *Nothing works!*
> *But I know how to blow apart those smirks.*
> *Game time is near*

And I'm number one.
I can't wait for all of you...
To face your opponent—my gun.

My grandfather's gun, old but shiny, had become a welcome friend of mine. It was almost too big to fit inside my backpack, but I had managed to get it in last year so I knew I could this time too. Sliding it inside, I zipped the pack, placing it on the bed next to my clothes and shoes.

The time had finally come.

Game time.

Chapter
Fifty-Two

Amanda

I was literally fuming as I rode the bus again to school. Still no calls from Detective Simms. That asshole was avoiding me!

I took my seat in the back of the bus, watching out the rear window as Dakota pulled away in her Cavalier.

And screw her too! She's treating me like I killed someone, instead of making a mistake!

Winter tried to talk my ear off in chemistry lab. I nodded, saying the appropriate "oohs" and "aahs," all the while my mind was somewhere else.

I had to go see Detective Simms today after school. I had to set the record straight once and for all to make sure he understood the truth—Sydney was innocent.

All Winter could talk about was getting fitted for uniforms. "Do you think we'll get our pompoms

181

today too?" she asked.

"I don't know," I practically growled at her.

I walked with Winter to second period—Brit Lit—avoiding Dakota's glare as I entered. Expecting her to ignore me as usual, I was surprised when she plopped down in Sydney's empty seat in the back, right beside me.

"I talked to Sydney last night," she said, smiling.

"You did?" I asked, mouth gaping open. "Is she okay?"

"She is. And she made me promise to stop being mad at you, even though I want to be mad at you still."

Dakota looked at me, her lips pouty. But then they curled up on the edges, the smile of a familiar friend.

"They're letting her out. Due to lack of evidence. And I'm pretty sure Coach Davis will let her back on the team," Dakota said.

I wasn't so sure about that last part, but I was happy to hear Sydney was getting out. I let out a sigh of relief. For the first time in weeks, I felt some weight release from my shoulders…finally things could get back to normal. *Sure, there was still a psycho on the loose, but at least that psycho wasn't my best friend.*

I said, "I know she's innocent. And I'm really sorry. I just jumped the gun—"

"Gun!" someone screamed from somewhere outside the classroom.

For a minute, it took my brain to register…

"He has a gun!" someone else screamed from down the hallway. I exchanged confused glances with Dakota.

Two gunshots rang out, followed by dozens of screams. People were running down the hallway!

My heart leapt into my chest, my body paralyzed with fear. I stared at Dakota. She was wearing a mask of pure terror.

"Everybody! Get under your desk and take cover!" Coach Davis shouted, running over to close our classroom door.

But before she could make it, there was a loud bang. I watched Coach Davis soar across the room, a baseball-sized hole in her gut.

Chapter
Fifty-Three

The shooter stood in the doorway, dressed in all black, a ski mask covering his face. Two piercing eyes moved side to side—it was all I could see through the mask.

Students were screaming, huddling up in the back of the classroom. Some of them were crying.

Some of them were praying…

I got down on the floor behind my desk, holding as still as possible. From here, I could see the shooter's bottom half as he came further inside the room and walked toward us, making his way through the aisle.

I flinched at the sound of another loud bang. More screams rang out.

Had he shot someone else?

Oh God, Coach Davis is dead…

I placed a hand over my mouth and nose, trying not to scream or cry out. Looking sideways, I met eyes with Dakota. Like me, she was on the floor behind her desk.

I've never been this scared in my life.

Dakota placed a finger to her lips, telling me to be quiet. Then she pointed her finger toward the doorway.

Surely, she wasn't suggesting that we try to make a run for it...

But then I remembered something that I heard once...that if you're ever being kidnapped at gunpoint, you have a better chance of living if you make a run for it than if you let the kidnapper take you.

Decidedly, I nodded at Dakota.

I could hear movement near the back of the room. "No, please don't!" one student said.

We have to go now while we're closer to the door than he is! If we don't get help, we'll all die! I realized.

I mouthed the word "now" to Dakota, and we both took off running for the door, sounds of gunfire ringing out behind us.

Chapter Fifty-Four

I hoped and prayed that all of those miles Coach Davis made us run would pay off. We sprinted down the hallway, making a quick right down an adjacent, shorter hallway.

The halls were eerily empty, students hiding and silent in their individual classrooms.

Heavy footsteps echoed down the hallway.

The killer was following me and Dakota!

I need to call the police! Horrified, I realized my cell phone was in my backpack—and my backpack was still in the classroom, under my desk. Useless to me…

Dakota and I stood frozen, not moving. Maybe not even breathing.

And that's when we heard it…there was a voice shouting—no, not shouting. *Chanting.*

"One. Two. Three. Four.
Knock those Dragons on the floor!"

The killer was coming!

"Five, six, seven, eight.
You can run like rabbits, but it's too late."

"In here," I whispered to Dakota, yanking her further down the hall, slipping inside my Child Development classroom. The room was empty this period. I closed the door to the classroom as quietly and quickly as possible, my heart thumping in my chest.

Dakota immediately dove behind Mrs. Brooch's desk, crawling up underneath it. Making a quick decision, I ran for the closet.

I'd seen the inside of it a few times. It was a huge walk-in space, filled with plastic dummy dolls, including the artificial infants, as well as CPR mannequins.

Darting inside the closet, I dove beneath a stack of dolls, holding my breath and keeping as still as possible.

In the quiet, I could hear footsteps only a few classrooms away—heavy footsteps, the killer's boots—and then suddenly, another gunshot went off. The gun was close, only one or two classrooms away.

My entire body tensed up and I willed myself not to move a muscle.

What would I do if the killer found me? I thought about my mom and grandma. I thought about all my friends. Oh God, please let them be safe…

Now the killer was whistling, footsteps sounding

closer and closer to us...

I took one deep breath and held it, praying that the killer just moved past us.

There's no reason to call her "the killer" anymore...I already recognized her voice.

Chapter Fifty-Five

"Come out, come out, wherever you are!" The killer stepped inside the classroom. Walking slowly, she moved past the big chunky tables. I could hear her steady feet moving as she kicked aside chairs and anything in her path.

"How about a game of Marco Polo?" she taunted. I squeezed my eyes shut, wishing for this to be over.

"There you are, Dakota!" My heart literally froze in my chest. "Get up on your feet! I'm going to enjoy this part!"

I could hear Dakota whimpering, begging the shooter not to kill her. I had to do something.

I *had* to do something.

I jumped up from where I was ducking and came running out of the closet, holding one of the plastic CPR dummies in front of me like a shield.

"Don't do it! Take me instead." I was out of the closet, now face to face with the shooter.

189

She was holding the gun pressed to Dakota's head, peering at me through the ski mask with bright green eyes.

Dakota's eyes were closed, her body shaking. I'd never seen someone so scared before...

"Let her go," I pleaded.

The killer laughed. "Now *why* would I do that?"

She pressed the gun harder against Dakota's temple. Dakota whimpered in pain.

"Because this is crazy. You don't really want to hurt anybody, do you?" I asked.

Another maniacal laugh. I had to admit—my question was stupid.

I took a few steps forward. "Please, just let Dakota go."

"Again, why would I do that? Especially considering the fact that I plan on killing you both?"

"Because Sydney was charged with the murder. No one even suspects it was you," I suggested desperately, gripping the mannequin so tight that my fingernails were digging into the artificial skin.

"You must think I'm stupid. I know they're letting her out. I know my plan didn't work, and I didn't even make the team..."

Out of nowhere, Brittani Barlow came charging through the classroom door.

"Not this time, you don't!" Brittani screamed, holding a serrated knife in her hand as she ran.

I don't know what was more frightening— Brittani Barlow with a maniac's knife or the masked killer holding the gun.

The killer, I decided instantly.

"Ahhhh!" Brittani screamed, charging straight at

the shooter.

The killer was so surprised by Brittani that she stumbled back, releasing Dakota. But then she got her bearings and aimed the gun at Brittani's chest right as Brittani lifted the knife. She pulled the trigger.

Chapter Fifty-Six

I motioned for Dakota to come toward me, but she stood wide-eyed and frantic, staring at Brittani's slumped body on the floor.

Brittani tried and failed, but I wouldn't. Her sneak attack had inspired me and given us a bit of momentum.

As soon as the killer reached down to grab Dakota again, I ran for the gun. I grabbed and tried to yank it from her hands. My hands were around it, but she wasn't letting go!

I fell backwards, still gripping the gun. But the killer was gripping it too, and now she was on top of me.

We wrestled for it, and then a loud bang went off.

It was so loud my ears shook—at least that's how it felt.

Am I shot?

I wasn't sure, but I kept fighting, butting my

head against the killer's head angrily.

And then suddenly, Dakota was jumping on the killer's back, screaming and fighting as she ripped at her back and head.

Suddenly, she let go, falling back. Leaving me with the gun in my hand.

Jumping to my feet, I aimed the heavy shotgun at Mariella Martin.

"Take off your mask," I demanded. Red curls hung down around her face, the mask halfway off from the struggle.

She shook her head. "You won't shoot me. You're not like your father, Amanda. You're not a killer. I'm walking out of here and no one is going to stop me."

Mariella moved for the door, but Dakota moved to stop her. In an instant, Mariella reached out and grabbed Dakota, wrapping her hands around her neck. She began squeezing Dakota's throat as hard as she could.

Dakota fought and kicked, but Mariella's grip was too tight.

Dakota's face turned red, almost purple...

"Let! Her! Go!" I screamed over and over, aiming the gun at Mariella's head.

But she wouldn't. She was going to kill my best friend!

I took a deep breath and pressed the trigger, watching Mariella's head blow apart.

The gun crashed to the floor.

"I'm not my father. He killed good, innocent people. I only kill bad guys," I whimpered, falling to the floor.

Chapter Fifty-Seven

Nobody knows why she did it, exactly.

Is it ever truly possible to understand the mind of someone like Mariella Martin? I don't know. I wish I could understand it because then maybe we could prevent others from turning into her…

But this isn't a perfect world. Like my mom once told me—*People are complicated.*

Mariella wanted to be a cheerleader. She wanted to be popular. She wanted it so bad she was willing to kill for it.

Why would she do this to us? To herself?

It was something I couldn't wrap my brain around, and maybe I'd never want to.

I never wanted to understand someone like Mariella Martin. I just hoped there weren't any more out there like her…

Chapter Fifty-Eight

Two Weeks Later...

The Harrow Dragon cheerleaders were lined up side by side, facing center court, looking toward the basketball goal.

But this wasn't game night.

We stood hand in hand, memorializing those lost in the shooting. Blakely Clovers and Brittani Barlow were dead. Blakely got caught in the crossfire when she was in the hallway. I didn't know her well until now. I felt bad for hitting her, wishing I'd gotten to know her and given her a chance to know me...

And I never thought I'd respect Brittani Barlow, but in all actuality, her actions that day saved our lives...

Apparently, she'd been so freaked out by the attack against her, she'd been carrying a knife to school. That was a troubling thought...

The gym was silent as everyone paid their respects. The center of the floor was adorned with memorial portraits, flowers, and letters all left by students. Principal Barlow stood off to the side of the gym by herself, her face contorted in pain over the loss of her only daughter. My heart hurt for the poor woman.

Coach Davis moved across the gym floor, pushing herself in a wheel chair. Coach Purnell tried to step in and help her, but she swatted him away. That was no surprise to me. Even after losing the ability to walk, she was one of the toughest ladies I knew.

Despite Mariella's sick, twisted games and evil plans—there were still so many good people, those who were here to mourn their lost classmates, even Mariella.

Her face wasn't on a memorial portrait, but I think we all felt her loss that day. She was a bad person who did horrible things, but what happened to her—all of us—was terrible and tragic.

I don't think I'll ever get over shooting her. I'd like to say that I'm brave and I did what I had to do, but still—it changed me. It made me darker inside—a gray space left in place of a small part of me that used to be pink and happy and trusting of the world.

Dakota was on my right and she gripped my hand. I smiled at her tightly, struggling not to cry. Sydney was in the stands, watching. She smiled and nodded at me too.

I know she's forgiven me, but I still feel bad. Mariella framed Sydney and I just fell right into her trap by believing her. But so did a lot of people, including the police...

Maybe if the police weren't focused on Sydney, they would have been out looking for the real killer—Mariella Martin. But it was too late to dwell on "what-ifs" now.

Sydney was locked up during tryouts, but Coach Davis had agreed to let her be an alternate. She was dressed in her uniform, but stayed on the bench while the rest of us stood.

Winter was on the other side of Dakota, gripping her hand tightly, but not by Dakota's choice. I doubt they will ever be friends.

"Are you okay?" Ashleigh asked me. She was standing on my left side, dressed in her full uniform. She was only an alternate, but now that Blakely and Brittani were gone, she and Gabriella got permanent spots on the team. *Lucky them.*

"I'm fine," I said quietly, staring straight ahead.

I still don't trust that girl...

***

It seemed wrong—watching students move the memorial flowers and stands off of the gym floor afterwards, clearing space for the dance floor. Our annual dance was scheduled tonight, and despite some teachers' insistence that it be postponed, Principal Barlow, for whatever reason, wanted the show to go on.

"It's what Brittani would have wanted," she had said.

The DJ booth was set up, as well as tables for

snacks and refreshments. The once bright lights of the memorial were now dimmed, perfect for couples who wanted to engage in some romantic dancing.

All of the girls who hadn't changed into dresses yet—like the cheerleaders and band members who were part of the memorial service—now hurried to the locker room to get ready for the big dance, including me. I've never been one for taking long to get ready, so I slipped into my dress and hurried back out to join the others.

Sydney came out of the girl's locker room. She was wearing a long, green, A-lined scoop dress, and as usual, she looked long and elegant, like a model who could own the runway. Dakota's dress was short and sexy, with tiny purple sequins and a poufy skirt far above the knees. Even though she was naturally short, her heels made her look as tall as Sydney. I admired my two best friends. They looked absolutely lovely.

Grandma Mimi had leant me a fancy mermaid dress, with a long lean waist with a wide poof at the bottom. It was bright red and showy, something I normally wouldn't wear. But I felt almost glamorous as I channeled my inner showgirl—my inner Mimi, I suppose...

Lauren's dress was the most eye catching, with sheer rainbow colored fabric and a skirt as poufy and long as a wedding train. She strutted out of the locker room, basking in her own glory, surrounded by her freshman posse.

The first song that came on was a slow one, and I wasn't surprised one bit to see Dakota and Andy heading out to the dance floor first. They moved liked they lived in their own little world, not caring who saw or joined them. Honestly, they really were a great couple.

Other couples and singles filled up the floor. I immediately noticed Jordan, pulling a tall brunette out on the dance floor—not his girlfriend, Lauren, I noted. I looked around for Lauren in the crowds again, expecting to find her upset somewhere or on the sidelines watching her cheater boyfriend.

But honestly, she too looked happy to be rid of that jerk. She was standing with her group of freshman girls, a couple I recognized from the squad, and she seemed to be having fun without him. Maybe she was happy to be rid of his flirtatious, cheating ass. I know I was.

Even Sydney, who was normally more concerned with her studies and cheerleading than boys, seemed surrounded by people and relishing in the attention. Ever since her arrest and falsely accused crimes, she had been getting showered by attention from guys and girls. She moved across the dance floor, locking arms with a dark-haired senior boy I'd never seen before till tonight.

Usually quiet, Sydney seemed to be coming out of her shell and enjoying her newfound freedom. I still had not asked her how rough it was in juvie. But Sydney was tough, and honestly, she was used to being alone—so my guess is that she handled it like a champ, the way she did most things in life.

After filling my cup with punch, I made my way around the edges of the dance floor, smiling at my happy friends as they danced and enjoyed the dance. It was a day for mourning, but also a day for celebration—we were finally free of the sociopath. I saw many classmates I had never noticed before. After what happened with the shooting...everyone seemed important and I was making an effort to learn all of the students' names at Harrow High.

For the first time in a long time, I felt safe again. The school shooting gave me a newfound lease on life. I wanted to be alive. And suddenly, all of the small stuff—like cheerleading and everyday drama amongst friends and peers—seemed so unimportant and dumb. I just wanted us all to be safe and happy, and that didn't seem like too much to ask.

I noticed one of my friends sitting in the bleachers, head hung down and quiet. I crept toward her, climbing up rows of seats to sit beside her.

"Winter, are you okay?" I asked. I smoothed the long layers of my dress, taking a seat beside her.

When she looked up, I could tell she had been crying. Her hooded black makeup was smudged on her pale white cheeks and below her eyes. Her white-blonde hair looked even whiter than usual with her all-white, sparkly dress.

Even when she was crying and looked like a total wreck, she was beautiful.

When she didn't answer my question, I said, "You look really pretty."

"Thanks," she said finally, sniffling. Her eyes drifted to the dance floor, where she glumly watched Andy and Dakota dancing.

I groaned. "Not him again," I teased, nudging her. "She will kick your ass if she sees you staring at him. You know what a pain Dakota can be sometimes."

Winter tried not to smile, but her lips were curving. "I know. But I just can't help it. I still have feelings for him, Amanda," she whined.

"What do you miss so much about dating him?" I asked, watching Andy playfully dip Dakota on the dance floor. They both looked so happy, and I didn't see Winter being able to break them up even if she tried.

"I guess I just miss the *idea* of him. We were like best friends when we were little and he was always infatuated with me. I guess I thought it would last forever, but then one day he moved on...before I really had a chance to tell him how much he meant to me."

I sat there quietly, unsure what to say, or what could make her feel better...

"And there are so many unpleasant memories and reasons to just let go of Andy, but I keep focusing on the good moments...the good memories I can't let go of," she said sadly.

I thought about her words, mulling them over. "You know I think I have the opposite problem with my dad. I focus on the bad so much, I can't seem to reach the good stuff anymore. When all I want to do is let the bad go, and just hold on to the good. I think it's good that it's in your nature to stick with the good—I do..."

Winter looked at me, wiping her nose. "I'm really sorry about what happened to your dad. Even if he made some bad choices, he did one thing right—he had you. And you're an awesome friend, Amanda. I'm so glad I met you this year."

We both smiled.

"You deserve a guy that likes you and who you like back. Maybe you and Andy were just meant to be friends, or even childhood sweethearts. You can let go of the good memories and focus on making new ones. With your new friends, and your new cheerleading team..." I said.

When she didn't answer, I nudged her.

"Yeah, you're right. I have a lot of things to look forward to this year. I'm just glad I'm not dead. I was so scared," she said.

"Me too," I said solemnly, remembering the jolt of shock that ran through my body when I heard the first gunshot.

It would take some time for us all to recover, that I knew for sure...

"Attention, please! Nominations are in for the Homecoming King and Queen. Quiet, everyone!" It was Mrs. Brooch on the mic. For someone usually so cranky, she seemed happy and animated tonight. I couldn't help wondering if someone spiked her punch. I stifled a giggle.

"Congratulations to this year's Homecoming King...Andy McGraw!"

The gym erupted with applause and cheers from students. A bunch of Andy's teammates on the basketball team were hooting and hollering their congrats. I smiled over at Dakota. She was beaming, so proud of her boyfriend.

"And now...for the moment everyone's been waiting for. This year's Homecoming Queen..."

I saw Dakota puffing out her chest, hoping she was the one. I also saw Lauren staring at the stage with a hopeful expression.

"The Homecoming Queen is our new girl…Winter Addams!"

The gym was filled with roars and whistles, students clapping for Winter.

"What?" She looked over at me to confirm this was true, looking truly in shock and awe.

I quickly wiped her tears away, trying to rub off some of the smudged black makeup, but to no avail. Winter stood up, still looking unsure of herself.

"Go up there," I said, nudging her. I watched her glide down the bleachers and make her way to the stage.

Meanwhile, I tried not to even look—Dakota was absolutely fuming. Suddenly, Sydney was beside me, grabbing my arm.

"We'd better get her out of here…she's so mad she might explode," Sydney said, talking about Dakota, of course.

I laughed despite myself. "Yeah, okay. Let's all get out of here. I'm thinking this day calls for more *Buffy* reruns and junk food!"

I felt happy for my new friend, Winter. Dakota would get over it. There was enough room at Harrow High for a few queens this year…

Chapter
Fifty-Nine

"I'm dying." It was the last thing I expected—or wanted—to hear from my Grandma Mimi on a day like today. We were sitting at the kitchen table, moments earlier having light conversation over bowls of spaghetti.

"What?" I dropped my fork, letting it fall and clang against the wood floor beneath me.

"I have cancer. And I don't have much longer to live," she said.

"I don't understand. You've been so happy lately, Grandma…why didn't you tell me sooner?"

"I didn't tell you because you had so much on your plate. But at this point, your plate can't get any fuller so I might as well tell you now," she explained.

My mouth was open. My heart hurt so bad I couldn't speak.

"Please don't be sad, Amanda. Even though I'm dying, for the first time I feel like I'm truly living. It may have taken me ninety years to figure it out, but I have. I don't want to waste one more second that I have with you. I love you, Amanda. I missed my chance to be a good mother, but at least I can be good to you before I die."

I dove out of my seat and ran around to hug my grandmother.

"Please don't die, Grandma…" I bawled into her chest.

"Baby, we're all dying. And life is too short. You saw that just the other day…when I nearly lost you…" Now she was crying too.

"You didn't lose me. I'm here, Grandma. Tell me what I can do to help. I'll take you anywhere you want to get treatment, and I'll take care of you…" I assured her.

"I don't want treatment. But I *do* want something."

I nodded, pleading her to give me something— anything—to do that would prove helpful to her.

"Let's go on a road trip, me and you. I want to show you Vegas. I want to show you the house your father grew up in, and I want to stand at the top of the Grand Canyon and feel alive—for however long that is…"

I nodded again, wiping tears and snot from my face. "Okay. I'm ready whenever you are, Grandma," I said, standing up straight.

"Well, I thought we could wait until the season was over. You need to be here for your games and such. But as soon as it's over, we'll head out West."

"The West is the best, or so I've heard," I said, smiling. "Let's leave tonight, Grandma. Let's just go. I'll drive you anywhere and everywhere you want to go. You'll never be hidden inside your house again."

"But what about cheerleading, honey?"

I smiled, thinking about Sydney. "That's what alternates are for."

***

The day before we planned to leave, I took the driver's test exam. Although I was willing to risk driving cross country without a license, Grandma Mimi wasn't. She said the only way she would let me drive is if I took the test and passed…

I missed two questions on the written part, and couldn't parallel park that big boat of a car to save my life, but somehow I passed anyway. "You passed by this much," the instructor said, holding up two fingers spread a millimeter apart.

As long as I passed, that's all that mattered…

I had spoken to all of my teachers and collected my assignments. I would have to do school work on the road, that way I didn't get too far behind on my studies. I didn't mind, and I knew Grandma Mimi would make me do it whenever I felt like slacking off…

I dropped off my cheerleading uniform and pompoms to Coach Davis's office. She was inside, sitting in her wheelchair at her desk, smiling despite her recent injuries.

"Will you ever walk again?" I asked her, placing the uniform and pompoms across her desk.

"I hope so. The prognosis looks good, but even if

206

I don't...I'm just lucky to be alive." I smiled.

That's a good way to look at it, I thought, smiling. We were *all* lucky to be alive.

When Grandma Mimi and my bags were packed and loaded up in the car, and as we pulled away from Harrow Hill, I told her that I had one last thing to do.

"It's not stopping to see that boy, is it? The one you had the baby with?" I rolled my eyes at "had the baby with."

"No, it's not him, Grandma. I want to stop and see my father."

She was quiet the whole way there, both of us deep in thought. "Want me to go with you or stay here?" she asked, as she pulled up and parked in front of the cemetery.

Unlike the other night when I came, the gates were open and the sun was shining, welcoming visitors.

"I need to do this alone," I said, slowly getting out of the car.

I took my time getting to my father's grave, not ready to say what I needed to say...

Finally, standing in front of it, my mind was blank...unsure what to say exactly.

"I still kind of hate you," I whispered. "But I remember so many things I loved...I loved the way you loved mom and me so fiercely. Sometimes it was too much, intense. I loved the way you made pancakes on weekends, and teased Mom relentlessly. I loved the way you called me Cookie, and always held my hand when we went somewhere. I loved how you always got up early in the mornings, watching me go off to school, even when you were tired. I loved you. I *still* love you.

I'm going to focus on the good stuff and try to let go of the bad. I'm going to try to make the most out of my time with Grandma Mimi. Like you, she's not perfect and neither is my mom. But maybe if I love them as fiercely as you loved me and Mom, I can help fix them. Or at least make them happy for a little while."

I knew it would be a while before I came to visit again. So I kissed the tips of my fingers, bent down and pressed them to the front of his grave.

"Good bye, Terrance Loxx."

Chapter Sixty

Ashleigh

As I walked inside my quiet, empty house, I couldn't help thinking about how beautiful the memorial service had been. I headed straight toward the stairs to the basement, feeling my way around in the dark until I reached the light switch.

I skipped the dance. There were lots of reasons to celebrate, but changing out of my uniform and into a dress didn't sound like much fun at all to me. I never wanted to take this thing off...

I stood in front of the full-length mirror, admiring my gorgeous new uniform. It felt like a dream come true. I couldn't wait to wear it on game night. I especially couldn't wait to wear it at the big competition in Dallas. The competition was bound to be killer...

"It wasn't a coincidence, was it? You killed Blakely and Brittani, making sure I got a spot on the team, just like I always wanted...and just like you said I would." Mariella was dead now, but somehow…I knew she was still listening to me. We will be friends forever—she said it herself in the note she sent me in juvie.

Sliding my hands up and down my sides, I grinned at my reflection, mouthing a silent cheer:

I hope it wasn't all in vain
I had a purpose but she was insane
I'll hold this team together, yes I will
And if anyone tries to stop me…
Kill Kill Kill

"See! I can make up poems too! Take that Mariella," I said, lifting my arms in a V.

The V was for Victory.

Acknowledgments

First and foremost, thank you to Shannon, Dexter, Tristian, and Violet for supporting my passions and rooting for me every step of the way.

Thank you to all of my fans and everyone who reads my books. I see all of your reviews and read all of your messages, and your feedback and comments mean more to me than you'll ever know. I couldn't do this without you.

Thank you in particular to my street team, Flocksdale's Finest. You guys are a fabulous group and I feel so lucky to have each and every one of you.

Thank you to my mother for always attending all of my games and being my biggest supporter, as a teen and an adult.

Thank you to all of the staff at Limitless Publishing who make it possible for me to write these stories. The fact that you believe in me, support me every step of the way, and allow me to share my books with the world is amazing. I'll be forever grateful.

Thank you so much to my incredible editor, Toni Rakestraw. She is patient and kind, and she's up in the middle of the night even on weekends helping me make my stories better. You're awesome, Toni! And I couldn't do it without you.

Thank you Ashley Byland of Redbird Designs for designing all of my Horror High and Flocksdale Files covers. You always surprise me and impress me with the ideas you come up with and the way you bring to life the characters who live in my head still amazes me! I don't know how you do, but you do it so perfectly!

Thank you to Mitsy Princell, for promoting my books, helping me organize events, and providing so much encouragement on a daily basis. It means more to me than I could ever express in words.

Thank you Mia of happianarky.com for helping me with my website and making teasers for me. Most importantly, thank you for being my friend. I can't wait for that trip to Nola we're always talking about.

Thank you to Lauren Delancey for being an awesome friend and fan, and for letting me use your name in one of my books.

Thank you to all of my family, friends, and fellow authors who provide so much emotional support and friendship to me on a daily basis. You guys inspire me to keep writing!

About the Author

Besides my family, my greatest love in life is books. Reading them, writing them, holding them, smelling them...well, you get the idea. I've always loved to read, and some of my earliest childhood memories are me, tucked away in my room, lost in a good book. I received a five dollar allowance each week, and I always—always—spent it on books. My love affair with writing started early, but it mostly involved journaling and writing silly poems. Several years ago, I didn't have a book to read so I decided on a whim to write my own story, something I'd like to read. It turned out to be harder than I thought, but from that point on I was hooked. I'm the author of *The Flocksdale Files Trilogy*, *This Is Not About Love* and *Grayson's Ridge*. I'm a total genre-hopper. Basically, I like to write what I like to read: a little bit of everything! I reside in Floyds Knobs, Indiana with my husband, three children, and massive collection of books. I have a degree in psychology and worked as a counselor.

Facebook:
https://www.facebook.com/CarissaAnnLynchauthor

Twitter:
https://twitter.com/carissaannlynch

Blog:
https://carissaannlynch.wordpress.com/

Goodreads:
https://www.goodreads.com/author/show/11204582
.Carissa_Lynch

Website:
http://carissaannlynch.com/